Timeless Love

Stella Gioacas

MAPLE
PUBLISHERS

Timeless Love

Author: Stella Gioacas

Copyright © Stella Gioacas (2022)

The right of Stella Gioacas to be identified as author of this work has been asserted by the author in accordance with section 77 and 78 of the Copyright, Designs and Patents Act 1988.

First Published in 2022

ISBN 978-1-915492-85-2 (Paperback)
    978-1-915492-86-9 (E-Book)

Cover Design and Book Layout by:
    White Magic Studios
    www.whitemagicstudios.co.uk

Published by:
    Maple Publishers
    1 Brunel Way,
    Slough,
    SL1 1FQ, UK
    www.maplepublishers.com

A CIP catalogue record for this title is available from the British Library.

All rights reserved. No part of this book may be reproduced or translated by any form or by any means, electronic or mechanical, including photocopying, recording or by any information storage and retrieval system without written permission from the author.

The book is a work of fiction. Unless otherwise indicated, all the names, characters, places and incidents are either the product of the author's imagination or used in a fictitious manner. Any resemblance to actual people living or dead, events or locales is entirely coincidental, and the Publisher hereby disclaims any responsibility for them.

Dedication

Timeless Love is dedicated to my lovely husband Razvan Gioacas who never let me give up my dream.

You are my pillar, my guide, my Timeless Love. xx

CONTENTS

Chapter 1

'I sure know how to pick them, don't I?' Emily said.

'Yep, you sure do, sweetie, and before you say anything, I did warn you about him.'

'I know, I know, you told me so. I'm just sorry I didn't listen to you,' she said, looking up at the sky. She didn't know whether she wanted to scream or cry, or do both!

'Argh, I just wasted two years of my fucking life with that man,' frustrated with herself and how her life had turned out.

She could feel the tears building up again and knew she had to fight them back down, because waking up this morning she had made a promise to herself, that she wouldn't waste a single tear on that man ever again. She had done enough of that last night, she thought to herself.

'I know honey,' putting her arm around her and pulling her in close.

'At least you found out now before it was too late.'

'You mean before I had a kid with him,' she said, more of a statement rather than a question. She knew exactly what she was saying because she was thinking the same thing.

'He's definitely not a man you want to be tied down to, that's for sure.'

This was Stacy, her best friend since childhood and that man - that vile, nasty, waste of space man - nearly destroyed their friendship, and the sad thing was that she let him.

Stacy had warned her about him, multiple times, even going as far as taking pictures of him with other women as proof. Because she knew he would somehow talk himself out of trouble as he always did. Sad, but true.

But what did the bastard end up doing? He turned it around and somehow convinced her that her own friend was jealous of her and their relationship, that she had tried it on with him and he had turned her down. That they were strong, soul mates and she shouldn't let anyone come between them and what they had.

What a fucking joke!

If she was Stacy, she wouldn't speak to her ever again.

The last time she saw her friend was months ago and she had actually accused her of wanting her man. How stupid she had been, how she believed his lies, how she allowed herself to get brainwashed by him.

You always see things like this in the movies, where you end up shouting at the telly and telling the woman to wake up and smell the coffee, while at the same time thinking that would never happen to you. Not realising how easy it was to get trapped in someone's web.

Well, now she knew because it had happened to her.

But if she was painfully honest with herself and the reason why she was so ashamed of herself, was that she wanted to believe his lies.

Deep down inside she knew the truth, but she had been so desperate for the perfect relationship, the happily ever after, a family of her own, that she chose to push it to the side and pretend that everything was perfect, when in reality it was anything but!

Unfortunately for her she was the only one who couldn't see it; of course everybody else could.

In the space of two years, he had managed to alienate her from all her friends and family. She even left her job because of him.

Fair enough, she had only worked at the bar in her local pub, no big loss there but it was still a job and it got her out of the house, but apparently, he didn't like the way the blokes would stare and flirt with her, said he wanted them to spend more time together.

More like he couldn't flirt with the local tramps when she was around.

In the end she left her job, hoping with her not working in the pub that he would come straight home to the flat they shared, after work instead of going for a drink, which he always said was because he didn't want to be home without her. Needless to say, it didn't go down that way.

Instead, she found herself most nights sitting alone, always watching the minutes ticking by on the clock wondering where he was and of course, every time she called, it would go straight to voicemail.

He would always come home around midnight stinking of booze. Most of the time he would simply pass out but if she dared say anything or ask where he was, he would start shouting, saying that she was suffocating him and that she wasn't his mother.

But she was his girlfriend, damn it! And deserved more respect.

She deserved better!

Eventually she realised that. Well, she had to. She couldn't exactly ignore the fact that she found him with some woman in their own bed! That would have been taking ignorance to a whole different level.

She shook her head now at the memory. The dirty tramp didn't even bother to at least pretend to be embarrassed or even to cover herself up, she just giggled.

Actually giggled!

And him, he just stared at her, blurry eyed.

She didn't even think he registered who she was, he really did look that drunk, not to mention, high as a kite. She knew this because the flat stank of weed.

But what bothered her the most was that the dirty little tramp actually had the cheek to wave at her and giggle 'bye', as she turned her back on them and walked away, quietly closing the door behind her.

How could any woman do that to another woman and in her own home? she wondered.

She couldn't say that she was entirely shocked by what she saw because deep down she knew he was a lying cheat. But she was numb, too numb, to yell and scream and scratch that little tramp's eyes out, which was what she should have done but instead had found herself walking straight to the local shop, where she bought a bottle of tequila and a pack of Bensons.

Standing outside the shop she lit up her first fag in six months, that first drag burning the back of her throat and chest, making her feel sick but good at the same time.

Another thing she had quit because of him. Fair enough it was a dirty, unhealthy habit and she was better off without it, but the reason she had quit in the first place was because he had led her to believe that he wanted to start a family with her.

She wasn't crazy, she wasn't baby mad. He was the one who brought up the subject of having a baby. He would even stroke her tummy and say he couldn't wait for his baby to be inside her.

It was moments like that, that made her want to believe his bullshit.

She thought they had wanted the same things, but she couldn't have been more wrong.

Towards the end she had become so desperate to get pregnant but for all the wrong reasons. She had thought that if she got pregnant, he would finally settle down, stop drinking and stop sleeping around.

But men like that never change, she was just so angry that it had taken her too long to realise that.

Tossing the unfinished fag away in disgust after a few puffs, she wasn't about to let that loser fuck up her health as well as her sanity.

So, with tequila in hand, she walked the thirty-minute walk to Stacy's and knocked on her door, not knowing if she would be welcomed. Not that she would have blamed her either.

The last time she saw her was a month ago and had accused her of being jealous and wanting Craig for herself. What an idiot she had been!

But Stacy had opened the door to her and welcomed her into her home with open arms.

And after a night of heavy drinking and crying in Stacy's arms, including throwing up on her bathroom floor because she couldn't stagger to the sink in time, here they now were, walking along in the local park behind Stacy's house.

Running her hand through the lavender shrubs as they walked past, and smelling her hand - she had always loved the smell of lavender and lily of the valley. But unlike the very fragrant lily, she had always found it amazing how certain types of lavender would only release their fragrance when crushed or after it rained.

Walking over to her favourite spot under a big, old willow tree, they sat down resting their backs against its big trunk.

Looking up and around at the curtain of the willow tree, it almost felt like they were sitting behind a green waterfall - what a majestic tree! she thought in awe.

If only they could talk and give their age-old wisdom like they did in the Disney movies she watched while growing up! She could have really done with that right about now, she thought, looking up at the clear blue sky through the waterfall of green.

Was it so much to ask for, for somebody to love you whole-heartedly for who you were, warts and all? Love you back how you love them? Obviously in her case it was.

Bumping shoulders with her and pulling her out of her depressing thoughts.

'Hey, chin up, sweetie, you deserve so much better than that prick,' Stacy said.

'And just remember there's someone out there for everyone, a soulmate waiting to be found.'

'Oh yeah? Well, I think mine's lost,' she said, making them both laugh.

Some things really do take saying out loud to realise how funny they sound.

'Where did you hear that crap from anyway?' she asked.

'Craig,' she said, looking at her and they both burst out laughing.

'It figures.'

Once the laughing had stopped the anger quickly creeped back in.

'Arh,' slapping her hands on her drawn-up knees.

'How could I have been so stupid!' she said, more to herself than to Stacy.

'Hey sweetie, don't be so hard on yourself. It happens to everyone, there's too many pricks in the world.' Putting an arm around her and drawing her in for a one-sided hug.

Which only ended up making her cry again, not because of Craig, these were guilt tears, she had been so horrible to her, and she had forgiven her, treated her like nothing had happened.

'I'm so sorry,' she said again.

'Hey... I told you, forget it, it's cool. I'm just happy that the truth came out and you're finally free of that creep. But don't get me wrong, I am not happy with how it happened.'

'I know.'

'When I get my hands on that bitch, I'm going make her wish she was never born, and him? I'm going to chop his balls right off,' getting animated with her hands.

Suddenly a thought entered her head and mixed with what Stacy had said about soulmates, she had to ask, 'Can I ask you something?'

'Sure honey, what is it?'

'Did he ever try it on with you?' she asked, feeling her heart beating frantically in her chest.

She was afraid she already knew the answer but still felt the need to ask the question and hear the answer.

'Yeah, it's when he started spouting all that crap about soulmates, I told him to sod off.'

'When?'

'I think it was about a month ago,' drawing her eyebrows together in concentration.

'Just before our argument?'

'Oh sweetie, it was never an argument. I knew it was him talking and not you,' giving her arm a reassuring squeeze.

The bastard had tried it on with her friend and when he got turned down, he came home accusing her of trying it on with him, trying to break up their friendship.

Trying to isolate her, trying to control her and it worked for a long time but not anymore, she had finally opened her eyes and saw him for the monster that he was.

No more was said after that, and they both sat there in their little green cocoon under the willow tree watching the ducks in the pond, the people going by, some on their bikes, some walking their dogs and others simply sitting around just like them, when suddenly a light lit up the sky.

Looking ahead she saw it had got considerably cloudy and lightning was streaking across the sky.

'They did say we were going to get a lightning storm today, but man, that came on suddenly. Come on, let's head back, we shouldn't be under a tree in weather like this,' getting up and brushing off her bum, like you do after sitting on grass, just to make sure you didn't sit in shit or have a big green stain on your arse, not like you could do much about it anyway.

They stepped out from under the cover of the willow tree and started to head off back, when suddenly not far from the tree, she heard a loud crack and everything around her went white, then nothing.

Chapter 2

Coming to, the first thing she noticed was the loud ringing in her head, it felt like her eardrums were going to explode right out of her ears, if that was even possible, and she felt utterly nauseous. Her whole body felt like it was trembling, but on the inside, like the very blood in her veins was vibrating.

It was so dark, and she could hear a voice, it sounded so near yet so far.

'Miss? Miss?'

'Mmm' just trying to move her hand to her stomach made her want to puke up.

'Miss? Are you ok? Can you open your eyes? Can you talk?'

Open my eyes? Is that why it was so dark? Did she pass out from all that tequila? But no, it couldn't be, that was last night, wasn't it?

Taking her brain a while to catch up, she heard that same voice again.

'Miss?'

It wasn't a voice she recognised, which made her want to open her eyes and quickly realised that was a big mistake. As she felt like she was falling down a deep black hole, managing just to turn her head to the side and open her mouth for all her stomach contents to come spilling out.

Slowly opening her eyes again and trying to move almost had her shouting out in pain, it felt like her body had gone through ten rounds with Mike Tyson.

What the hell had happened to her?

Realising she was lying down, she tried to sit up but quickly gave up that plan when the room started to spin and she saw that she was in a very tiny single bed, if you could call it single. It wasn't even a child's bed, her feet were literally touching the metal end.

Where was she?

Looking down at herself, she saw she was covered in dried puke. Oh shit, she thought, so that's what that nasty, sour smell is, all that bloody tequila.

Trying to shift position in the bed, she realised she was damp down there, oh god, please don't let it be true, she silently prayed inside her head.

Putting a hand down between her legs and pulling her hand back up, while knowing it definitely wasn't that time of the month. And slowing bringing her hand to her nose, she realised with horror that she had indeed, royally pissed herself.

Double shit!

What the hell is wrong with you? she thought, disgusted with herself.

Looking around the room and although her vision was still very blurry, she definitely didn't recognise the place. It wasn't her flat or Stacy's for that matter, so where the hell was she? Looking around, she saw how bare the room almost was. Apart from the tiny bed she was currently lying in, on the right, there was a small-sized, slim desk up against the wall by the door, with a small wooden chair pushed in, with a standing coat hanger beside it next to the door. On the left was a two-door wooden wardrobe that also looked quite small, definitely not your standard wardrobe. Maybe they shopped in IKEA, she thought when she suddenly heard voices coming from the other side of the door.

She couldn't make out what they were saying as it sounded like they were whispering, but she could definitely tell that they were both men.

Panic was now starting to settle in, where the hell was she and where was Stacy?

The last thing she could remember was being extremely hung over, ok maybe a little bit drunk too, considering how much she had to drink, but she was fine, even went for a walk in the park with Stacy. So, what the hell happened after that?

Did she pass out?

But that still didn't explain where Stacy was, she wouldn't have just left her, unless she was in the care of doctors in a hospital, and this didn't look like a hospital.

With a sinister thought gradually creeping into her mind. Oh my god! Had she been kidnapped? She thought, had Stacy been kidnapped? Was she here too?

The thought had her trying to sit up but in doing so nearly puked up on herself again, ok… definitely not ready for any sudden movements.

Just at that moment she heard a noise and turned just in time to see the door slowly opening and a man walk in. She did consider closing her eyes and pretending to still be asleep, but her fuzzy brain was so slow she didn't even finish thinking it and the man was already by the bed looking down at her.

'You're awake, Miss, how are you feeling?' he asked, with what sounded strangely like concern in his voice.

Well, she was no expert, but he didn't sound like a kidnapper and neither did he look like one. But hey, what did she know?

The first thought that had entered her head when seeing him, was that he looked like he belonged in the Mary Poppins film.

He was tall and well built, not overly muscular like the type at the gym but more naturally toned. He was wearing a white shirt that was no longer the white it used to be and navy blue trousers with straps attached, which went over his shoulders and looked like they were supposed to be holding them up like a belt. What the hell were those things called? Garters? No, that wasn't it. That was going to bug her now, she thought to herself.

'Miss? Are you alright?'

Looking up at his face, she saw he had a gentle look about him with honey blond hair cut short and a light brown beard, but not the long scruffy type, this one was kept short and neat. And he had the most striking hazel-coloured eyes she had ever seen, which looked orange in the sunlight streaming in through a window behind the bed, which she hadn't noticed until now.

'Erm, yeah I'm fine,' she said, after clearing her throat.

'Miss, with all due respect but you took quite a hit, and you are still very pale,' drawing his eyebrows together in a frown.

'Would you like some water?' he asked.

'No thanks, I'm fine.'

Well, she wasn't fine, there was a loud ringing in her head and the pain was so bad it felt like her head was about to explode, with pieces of her brain flying everywhere. Not to mention that she really wanted to puke up again, but she wasn't about to admit that to a stranger, no matter how nice he seemed.

Putting a hand to her temple and applying some pressure to relieve the pain.

'Where's Stacy?' she asked, not looking at him as the sunlight shining on his face from the window was really hurting her eyes. So, she decided it was best to keep her head down and make minimal movements as much as possible.

'I'm sorry Miss, but you were alone when I found you.'

At this her head snapped up in his direction, that's impossible she thought. Stacy wouldn't have just left her. She knew she had been a bit of a bitch with all that Craig business, but they had sorted that out, hadn't they?

She wouldn't just leave her, would she? Especially when hurt. No, something must have happened or maybe she went to get help, but then wouldn't she have just used her phone? Maybe her battery died, she thought.

All these questions were going through her head at such a fast pace, that she started to feel like she was on a merry go round.

Turning her head just in time, she puked up on the floor beside the bed with a little bit going on her pillow, well at least it wasn't all over herself this time or on the man's boots, who she just noticed, was wearing black wellington boots.

Rather than stepping back, he moved closer to her bedside and produced a handkerchief from his pocket, handing it to her to wipe her mouth.

For a second there it looked like he was going to wipe her mouth for her, but then drew back his hand and handed it to her instead.

When she was done wiping her mouth and chin, he handed her a glass of water which she took a sip from and handed back to him. She was actually very thirsty, but her hands felt so shaky she was afraid of dropping the glass. She didn't need any more embarrassing moments, puking up and pissing herself was enough for one day.

'What do you mean I was alone?' she asked.

'You were alone Miss,' he stated again.

'Try and get some rest, Miss, the doctor will be back tomorrow morning to check on you.'

'The doctor?' Nothing he was saying was making much sense.

'Yes, Miss, the doctor just left. He examined you, with a chaperone, of course,' he added quickly.

'He said your pulse is a little fast but that is to be expected after getting hit by lightning, and you may suffer from headaches, blurry vision and sickness, but of course all this is to be expected… Miss, are you ok?'

Did he just say hit by lightning? If only this ringing in her head would stop, it was driving her mad and she couldn't think straight.

'Which hospital am I in?'

'You're not in a hospital, Miss, the hospital is an hour away and I didn't know how bad a condition you were in, so I brought you here to my room and got the local doctor to come round, instead.'

Putting her hands to her ears, she pressed hard hoping to dial down the ringing. She barely heard a word of what he had said, she just wished this ringing would stop!

'You could have just called 999 you know,' she said, a little too loudly because her hands were still on her ears.

'What's 999?' he asked, pulling his eyebrows together in confusion. Maybe he should bring the doctor back he thought, he did say she took quite a hit to the head when she hit the ground.

'Are you serious? What's 999? Are you winding me up?' she asked in disbelief. What was wrong with this guy?

Seeing the blank look on his face, she continued, 'You know the numbers you dial on your phone when you need help, and in my case an ambulance,' punching her finger in the air as if to show him how it's done.

'A phone?'

'Yeah, a phone. You know one of those things that you carry around with you, fits in your pocket and you can make calls, send texts, emails, even watch Netflix nowadays.'

Christ, he looked confused.

'Netflix?' he asked, tilting his head slightly.

'Oh my god! What are you? Amish?' almost yelling in frustration.

Did he not understand anything she was saying? She was pretty sure they were speaking the same language because she could understand everything he was saying, unfortunately.

Putting his hands in his pockets, 'No, and I think I should get the doctor back because you're clearly hallucinating,' he said.

She was starting to get really annoyed now, the cheek of him to say she was hallucinating! This man was standing by her bedside, basically telling her he had found her unconscious and decided to just bring her here to his room, instead of taking her to a hospital. And to top it all off, she didn't think she could even move, so she wouldn't even be able to defend herself if she needed to. Let's hope she didn't need to.

'Just call my friend please,' she said pleading with him.

'Where does your friend live and what's her name? I can get a message to her.'

'Just call her, her number's in my phone.'

'Miss, I don't know what this thing you're talking about is, but if...'

She didn't let him finish, finish what exactly? For crying out loud.

Her head felt like it was about to explode.

'A TELEPHONE, where are you from, the Middle Ages!'

'Well, I don't think 1874 is classed as the Middle Ages.'

Wait what? What did he just say?

Feeling something warm and wet tickling her ear, she put a finger to it and bringing her hand back down, saw it had blood on it. Blood was coming out of her bloody ear!

At this point the room began to spin again and she had the strangest feeling of pins and needles in her cheeks. The last thing she saw before her eyes rolled back and she passed out, was the man's face over hers.

Once the doctor left for the second time that day, Henry found himself sitting in a chair beside the bed watching her sleep, and not because he had nowhere to lie down as she was in his bed, but because he was genuinely worried.

He had found her hurt and unconscious, it was his duty to make sure she would be ok and make sure she was once again reunited with her family.

She looked so scared and confused when she woke up, he didn't want her waking up alone again.

But who was she? That was the question deep in his thoughts for hours now, among many others.

Everything about her was strange, for one, what on god's green earth were those clothes she was wearing? He'd never seen a woman wearing men's trousers before and they were certainly not any trousers he had ever seen before either.

And what was that she was wearing on top? Was it some kind of undergarment?

And he wasn't even going to start questioning her shoes, or that strange thing that fell out of her pocket when he had carried her in and laid her down on the bed.

Honestly if she didn't have long hair and a shapely figure, he would have thought it was a man he found unconscious and not a woman.

Another question that was on his mind was how she had even ended up in the fields in the first place, he could have sworn there was no one else around at the time.

Too many questions and no answers but there wasn't much he could do about it, not until she woke up at least.

Leaning back in the chair and folding his arms, he closed his eyes and decided to try and get some rest, because it looked like tomorrow was going to be a long day.

Chapter 3

Feeling the light behind her closed eyes, she slowly opened them and saw that the light was coming through the little window above her head.

Turning her head slowly to her right, she saw the man from yesterday sitting in a chair fast asleep. Did he stay by her side all night? Or maybe it was still the same day, and she hadn't been sleeping that long, she wondered.

Pulling herself up into a sitting position, she was happy to notice that the movement didn't make her want to puke her guts out again. The headache however was another matter, that was still painfully there but she could cope with that. What she couldn't cope with was the nausea, she had always had a fear of throwing up, ever since she was a kid.

She considered waking him up by touching his arm or coughing or something, but in the end decided against it.

Instead, she took this opportunity to look around the room, more closely this time as the last time she was still very dazed and confused, not that she wasn't still confused but at least she wasn't dazed.

She was grateful to see that her pillow had been changed after she puked on it and she was thankful to the man for obviously looking after her, but she needed to go home, not to mention the fact that she desperately needed to wash and change her clothes, she absolutely reeked.

Well, what do you expect when you puke and piss on yourself, to smell of roses? she thought to herself.

She also needed to know what had happened and who he was and most importantly why he decided to bring her here, wherever here was, instead of getting her to a hospital.

That was the bit that concerned her the most, any normal law-abiding citizen would have called for help, not taken her to their room in God knows where.

She vaguely remembered part of their conversation earlier, where he mentioned the hospital being an hour away. Well, that just didn't make sense because she knew the hospital was a twenty-minute drive away and that was in traffic!

No, something definitely wasn't right here, and she had to tread carefully.

Remembering her phone, she shifted on to her side and felt for it in her back pocket where she always put it and realised it was gone. Did she lose it, or was it taken?

She really wished she had her phone so she could check the time, she hated not knowing the time or date. She was the type of person who if ever witnessed a crime, she would be able to tell the police the exact hour and minute it occurred. Craig always called her the time police, she remembered with a sour taste in her mouth.

Turning back to look at the man beside her, she nearly jumped out of her skin to see him wide awake, in the same position but just quietly watching her.

Swallowing down a huge lump that suddenly formed in her throat, 'You nearly gave me a heart attack,' she said, putting a hand to her frantically beating heart.

'I do apologise, Miss. I didn't want to startle you by speaking suddenly, so decided to stay quiet instead,' giving her a sheepish smile.

'Yeah, next time just speak,' she snapped.

He couldn't help but chuckle at the way she said that. 'Hand on heart, next time I'll speak,' he said, putting his own hand to his chest.

'How are you feeling today?'

So, she had been right, it was a new day. 'A lot better, thank you,' she said, looking around the room, then back at him sitting in the chair. 'Did you erm… did you stay here all night?' she asked, feeling embarrassed and kind of worried too.

Was he just watching out for her or was something more sinister going on? Maybe she watched too many stalker movies, she thought giving herself goose bumps.

'Yes, Miss, you were very unsettled, tossing and turning, and it sounded like you were in pain, but you settled halfway through the night though.'

'Oh,' was all she could think of to say right now.

She still wasn't quite sure whether she should be thanking him for saving her life or running for her life.

'The doctor will be here soon to check up on you, would you like something to eat?' he asked, as he poured her a glass of water from a jug which was on a small round mahogany table next to the bed beside his chair and handed it to her.

And that was another thing, this doctor, she had never seen him. She heard him speaking to somebody yesterday and heard another man's voice but how could she know if that was a doctor? Could have been his accomplice for all she knew.

'Erm, I'm fine thanks. If you can get me an Uber that would be great,' she said after downing the glass that was handed to her.

'To eat? Is that some kind of meat?' pulling his eyebrows together in confusion and not for the first time.

Oh my god! What was he on? Did she hear him right? Her ears were no longer ringing, but did they get damaged somehow and she was hearing things, or did he really just ask her if she wanted to eat an Uber?

This guy must be smoking some strong shit, she thought to herself.

They both watched each other in awkward silence for a few moments, until there was a knock on a door somewhere in the house, if it was a house, she thought. The knock sounded distant; it could be a warehouse for all she knew.

Getting up and putting the chair he had been sitting on back by his desk, 'that would be the doctor,' he said, smiling awkwardly and closing the door behind him as he left, presumably to go answer the door.

Maybe she should be afraid, she thought to herself. But somehow, she just couldn't feel afraid. Maybe she was being stupid or that bang on her head really did do some damage, but she always trusted her instincts and right now her instincts were telling her that this wasn't a bad guy, despite all the weirdness.

Well, let's be honest, you silly cow, you don't always follow your instincts now, do you? she told herself. Look what happened with Craig, she knew he was a lying cheat, felt it deep down in her gut but she chose to ignore it.

But she just couldn't bring herself to fear this guy, sure this whole situation was strange, the guy was strange, but it wasn't anything he had done. Well, apart from bringing her to his room.

But it was just the way he was, the way he dressed, the way he spoke and behaved... something felt off, she just couldn't put her finger on it.

Letting that thought trail off, she pulled the sheet back with the intention of getting out of bed and immediately wished she hadn't, quickly pulling it back up and patting down the sides. The stench that had travelled up to her nostrils nearly made her gag, it was that bad. That was when she remembered she had puked all over herself, looking down at her T-Shirt under the sheet she saw the evidence right there, all dry and crusty.

Not to mention she had also pissed herself, none of which she could remember doing.

Taking a few deep breaths to calm herself, she really wished she had her phone to call Stacy, find out what happened and hopefully get picked up. She just wanted to go home, eat and most of all have a bloody shower.

But where exactly was home? She definitely wasn't going back to the flat she shared with Craig, never again. Maybe Stacy would be ok with her staying a few nights, at least until she found somewhere to rent.

As she was thinking about what to do, she heard voices coming closer to the door, one she recognised and the other she presumed to be the doctor.

As she saw the door handle turning, she settled back and pulled the sheet up as high as possible in order to hide the sorry state she was in, and hopefully keeping the smell down.

Upon entering, she saw that the two men were not alone and that there was also a woman with them a few steps behind, and for obvious reasons, this made her feel slightly more comfortable and safe.

She was short and looked young, possibly late teens or early twenties, or perhaps she was older than she looked and could put it down to good genes, she thought.

What she did however find strange, was her outfit, and again Mary Poppins popped to mind, which seemed to be the theme around this place.

She was wearing a long black dress whose collar came up to her chin, and long sleeves with a white full-length gown over the top.

Coming further into the room to stand at the end of the bed.

'Good morning Miss, it's nice to see my patient finally sitting up,' the other man said with a warm smile.

So, this must be the doctor then, she thought looking down and seeing a very worn brown leather bag held in his hand.

He was a tall man and very overweight in her opinion. He was wearing black trousers with a long black coat on top that was far longer on the back then the front, with what looked like a white shirt underneath.

'How do you feel, my dear?' he asked gently.

'I feel much better, thank you. I still have a banging headache though,' she said, touching her temple.

'Any ringing in your ears?'

'No, not anymore,' she said shaking her head slightly.

'Good, good, how are you on your feet?' he asked.

'She hasn't done any walking yet sir, she just woke up not long now,' the guy said, before she had the chance to say anything.

She didn't quite like the way he spoke for her, even though it was what she would have said herself.

'Thank you, Henry,' the doctor replied, nodding his head in the guy's direction, who she now knew was called Henry.

'Well, let's check that bump on your head and have a little listen to your heart, and we'll see about getting you back on your feet.'

'That would be great, thanks.'

Thinking the sooner they get this over with, the sooner she could get the hell out of Amish town. I mean, look at what they were all wearing, she thought, looking from one to the other.

'Henry, if you may,' turning from her to face Henry and indicating with his hand towards the door, gesturing for some privacy.

'Yes sir,' he said, nodding his head and with that left the room closing the door behind him.

'Rose my dear, would you come and stand over here?' he said to the young woman standing by the door.

'Yes sir,' she said, and quickly came to stand by the end of the bed.

The doctor came round to her side and first had a quick listen to her heart, then checked her head which she found surprisingly tender when touched, as she didn't realise until now that she had a golf sized ball at the back of her head. Well, that explained the headache from hell then, she thought, wincing in pain.

'Everything seems well, my dear. I wouldn't worry too much about that lump,' he said, seeing her putting a hand to the back of her head. 'That would go down in a few days. Now, shall we get up and have a little walk, see if there's any dizziness?'

She was about to say, "Hell yeah," when she remembered she had peed herself. She didn't want to imagine what they would be thinking, seeing her walking around with a giant pee stain on her jeans. Does dry pee even show? she wondered.

'That's ok, I'm kind of tired still, must be this bump on the head. Maybe later,' she said, feeling embarrassed while knowing the doctor wasn't buying her lame excuse.

Sitting down on the edge of the bed and putting a gentle hand over hers, he gave her a warm and knowing smile.

'It's ok, my dear, we know. It's perfectly normal when you have been hit by lightning, it's lucky you survived with no serious injuries. That is what is important here.'

Leaning closer, he whispered, 'Besides, I have seen much worse.'

Well, when he put it that way. Looking towards the woman at the end of the bed, she saw her giving her a reassuring smile and nodding her head.

Taking a deep breath, she said. 'Ok, let's go.'

'Now, take it sl...'

Before he even finished speaking, she swung her legs over the bed and obviously stood up too quickly, as she soon found herself sitting back on the bed feeling like she was on a merry go round.

'I was going to say take it slow or you would get a dizzy spell.'

'Yeah, sorry. I guess I'm just desperate to get home.'

He simply patted her hand and said, 'Come on, let's try again, and this time slowly.'

She did as he instructed and managed to walk around the room a couple of times without getting dizzy.

Coming to sit back down on the bed, she bent to put her trainers on which she noticed were placed by the bed.

'Can I ask, what are those my dear?' coming to sit on the edge of the bed and pointing towards her feet.

'These? These are Nike,' she said, doing up her laces.

'An interesting name for shoes,' he said, looking at them as if he had never seen trainers before.

Seeing the look on his face she decided to clarify. If it was anybody else, like that Henry guy, she would have said something like, "Well dah, you've never seen trainers before?" but the doctor had been so nice to her, she didn't have it in her to be sarcastic with him.

'No, that's just the brand. These are called trainers.'

'Trainers,' he repeated, like he had just learnt a new word.

Turning back to the young woman, 'Rose, my dear, you can tell young Henry he can come back in now. I am sure he has been hovering outside the door,' he said, giving Emily a wink.

Rose went and opened the door and sure enough Henry was there waiting.

'Come in, Henry,' the doctor called.

'The young lady here is well and ready to go home.'

Oh, thank God, she thought to herself.

'Now my dear, if you tell us where home is, I am sure young Henry here will see to it that you get home safely.'

'That's ok, honestly you have done more than enough, both of you,' she said, looking back at Henry.

No matter how much of a weirdo she thought he was, she had to acknowledge the fact that he had looked after her.

Turned out he wasn't a kidnapper after all. Because even though she didn't admit it to herself, because the thought didn't bear thinking about, somewhere deep in the back of her mind she did wonder if maybe she had been kidnapped.

Almost laughing out loud at the thought, who the hell would want to kidnap her, her own boyfriend didn't even want her!

'If you can just call me a cab, that would be great. I would get an Uber, but I lost my phone.'

Henry and the doctor exchanged a look

'Are you sure she is well enough to leave, sir?' Henry asked with a raised eyebrow.

'She is quite well,' the doctor assured him, although Henry didn't look convinced.

Suddenly she got it, all the pieces of the puzzle finally slotted in to place, everything made sense now.

This was probably Stacy's idea of a joke, make her think she's in Amish town. Probably payback for all that Craig business, she had been quite a bitch to her.

Suddenly jumping up, she would have almost fallen over if the doctor hadn't put out a hand to help steady her on her feet.

'Ha, ha, very funny,' she said, throwing her arms up and looking around the room.

'You got me, where's the cameras?' she said, walking around the room and looking at the few pieces of furniture in the room, the walls, anywhere you could put a tiny camera.

'Come on Stacy, you can stop hiding now. I know you're here somewhere,' she called out.

But nobody came out of hiding.

'My dear, come sit down,' the doctor said, after a while.

'I don't want to,' she said, folding her arms across her chest.

She knew she probably sounded like a child having a tantrum, but she didn't care, she didn't like games and she certainly didn't like this one. After everything she had been through, she didn't think she deserved this.

Taking a sideways glance at the older man, she suddenly felt guilty for snapping at him, even if he was just acting.

Silently she went back to the bed and sat down beside him, sighing deeply.

'So, my dear...'

'You can call me Emily, my name's Emily,' she said in a small, defeated voice.

Giving her a nod, 'Emily, I was wondering if you would do me the honour of explaining to me what this phone is, that you keep speaking of.'

So, it's not just Henry, it's the doctor as well.

She seriously doubted the doctor would have agreed to be in on some prank, maybe they really were Amish after all, but then again, they would still know what a phone is, wouldn't they?

In any case, she decided it was just best to play along.

'Ok, a phone is a small device, roughly around this size...' showing him with her hands.

'Some are bigger, some are smaller depending on the make. And you can make calls, send texts, emails, take photos and even watch Netflix nowadays.'

'And this Uber you mentioned earlier?'

'Oh, I believe that's some sort of luncheon meat, sir,' Henry said, and she got the impression by the way he said it, that he was excited about knowing something the doctor didn't.

It was one of those, "Ah, bless" moments that she couldn't help but smile at.

'Actually, it's a cab.'

Looking back at the doctor, she explained. 'It's actually an app that you download on your phone. Whenever you need a ride, wherever you are, you just go on the app and request a cab. The driver then arrives, usually within minutes, picks you up and takes you where you need to go. Simples,' she said, shrugging her shoulders.

'What's an app?' They both asked at the same time.

Looking from one to the other, she was stunned. How could they not know anything? How isolated were they from civilization? Christ!

'It's a software application, app is short for application. You download it as I said on a phone, tablet, even a watch, one of those smart ones though, not just any old watch because it needs to have access to the internet,' she finished off, hoping she had explained it right.

Seeing them both just staring at her, oh god, she thought to herself, these people literally knew nothing about the modern world.

She really hoped she hadn't stumbled upon some weird cult.

And before they could say or ask anything else she said, 'And don't ask me what the internet is.'

They all went quiet for a while, with the doctor staring at a spot on the floor looking like he was deep in thought.

It seemed like ages before he finally spoke but in actual reality it was probably well under a minute.

'Emily, where did you get those clothes you are wearing? I have never seen a woman wearing a man's clothes before. But even these, my dear, I find very strange.'

'What? You can't be serious?'

Jesus Christ, these people needed to enter the 21st century! They were completely bonkers, she thought to herself.

'Oh, I am very serious, my dear.'

Looking at Henry, 'Henry, remind me again how you came across young Emily here,' he said.

'Like I said, sir, I had just finished working in the fields when the storm started. I was about to leave when I heard the lightning strike and I looked back and there she was, lying on the ground.'

'And what about you Emily, what do you remember?' he asked, looking at her now.

'Oh, I remember everything, even after all that tequila,' she said laughing, and then continued when they just stared at her.

'Anyway, I was in the park with my friend. I remember we were sitting under my favourite tree when the lightning storm suddenly hit out of nowhere. We then got away from the tree, because everyone knows you shouldn't be under a tree during a lightning storm. Anyway, we moved away from the tree and started to head back to Stacy's, then... Nothing, I guess that's when I got hit.'

'Who is this Stacy?'

'My friend,' she said.

'That's the person she was mentioning, sir,' Henry said.

'I see... And did you see anybody else around at the time you found her, Henry?'

She felt a moment of hope until it quickly vanished when Henry spoke.

'No sir, I was completely alone even before the storm hit. As I said earlier sir, one minute I was alone and the next there was this strange woman lying on the ground.'

'Hey... who you are calling strange?' frowning at him, how dare he call her strange, he was the strange one here, not her.

'Emily, my dear,' the doctor said drawing her attention back to him, 'Would you do me the honour of telling me what year it is?'

'It's 2022,' she said, rolling her eyes in frustration.

Henry who at that moment decided to have a glass of water, found himself spraying it out of his mouth and nose.

'Thank you for that, Henry,' the doctor said taking out a handkerchief and dabbing at his jacket.

'Sorry sir,' Henry said coughing.

'You alright there?' she asked, amused.

'Are you?' he asked, making her draw her eyebrows together.

Yeah, this guy was starting to piss her off, she thought.

'My God,' the doctor said in a whisper.

'What is it sir?' Henry asked.

The doctor momentarily looked at Henry but ignored him and turned back to face her.

'My dear, this is the year 1874!'

Chapter 4

'1874, are you serious?' she said on a laugh.

Getting up and walking around the room, were these people fucking mad? What the hell did she get herself into!

'Henry, where is this device you say fell out of her pocket?'

'It's here, sir...' going over to his desk and opening a drawer. 'I put it here for safe keeping.'

'Can I have a look?' the doctor asked, putting out his hand.

'Of course sir,' Henry said.

Hearing their conversation, she turned towards them and saw it was her phone.

'Hey, that's my phone,' she said, walking over and snatching it from Henry's hand, just as he was about to hand it over to the doctor.

'So, you did take my phone.'

'No Miss, this thing fell out of your pocket when I picked you up from the ground.'

She didn't know this man from Adam but for some reason she thought he might be telling the truth. If he wanted to steal her phone, he wouldn't have admitted taking it in the first place, now would he? she thought. Thieves usually deny taking things, don't they?

Well, the bottom line was that she couldn't be sure, so she had to tread carefully.

Turning it over in her hands she saw the screen was cracked, shit! she thought when the phone wouldn't come on.

Hopefully it wasn't broken, and the battery just died on her, maybe she could borrow a charger from someone.

'Emily, may I have a look?' he asked, reaching out his hand.

'Yeah, sure,' handing him the phone.

What harm could it do? she thought.

'It's probably broken,' she said, sitting back down on the bed next to the doctor, watching him turning it over in his hands.

'These phones weren't built to last long anyway, you drop them once and they shatter into a million pieces. Now the old ones in my opinion were the best ones, you could throw them against a brick wall and they would still work.'

'Why would you throw something against a wall?' Henry asked, clearly puzzled.

'I don't know... when you're angry, I suppose.' She remembered doing that once, but not with her phone, she wasn't that crazy; it was Craig's headphones after he failed to come home for dinner because the pub was more important.

If she was honest, she threw quite a few things against the wall, door, floor… during her time with Craig. But the satisfaction you get when smashing something in anger is always ruined afterwards when you have to get a dustpan and brush to clear it up.

'I have never seen anything like this,' the doctor said quietly, almost to himself and she wouldn't have heard him if she hadn't been sitting so close to him.

'What do you mean?' she asked, looking at him now.

She was starting to get a little worried now, these people looked like they were being serious, and their clothes, the room… looking around and taking everything in as if for the first time. Even their manners were different, could what he said be possible… but how?

It didn't bear thinking about.

'I mean, my dear, this device, this phone as you call it, doesn't exist yet.'

'Sir, how could this be possible?' Henry asked.

'I strongly believe that young Emily here…' pausing and looking up at her, 'has travelled here from the future,' he said.

And there it was, the bombshell that just shattered everything they all believed in.

They all went silent, obviously shocked at what the doctor had just said.

'But how?' was all she could say when she was able to speak again.

'I honestly don't know my dear,' he said, shocked himself, at what he had just discovered.

'But humans can't travel at the speed of light and that's what's needed right?' remembering that bit of information from secondary school.

'What do you mean, has this sort of thing been attempted where you're from?' Henry asked.

'No. Well, I don't know. To be honest, it's not like they tell us anything. I mean, if they can clone animals now, then who knows...' she said shrugging her shoulders.

'Clone?' he asked, obviously lost with what she was saying which was understandable all things considered.

She didn't even know where to begin explaining that one, but luckily, she didn't need to as the doctor stood. 'Emily, may I take this? To have a closer look?'

'Sure, why not?'

Not much she could do with it anyway, maybe while he was at it, he could fix it, she thought to herself.

'Rose, my dear, shall we?' he said.

She had forgotten Rose was still here in the room, she was so quiet standing to one side.

When he reached the door, he turned round and said, 'You should go out, get some fresh air, it will do you good.'

'Maybe you could take your sister out later,' he said looking at Henry now.

'Yes sir, I understand,' nodding his head.

'Very well, I will come by tomorrow.' And with that he left, quickly followed by Rose.

Leaving her and Henry alone again.

She wasn't exactly comfortable being left alone with this guy but from the looks of things, he didn't look so comfortable himself either.

Putting his hands in his pockets and rocking back and forth on his heels, his discomfort was loud and clear.

It was a good thing his trousers were being held up by those braces she thought, because he had his hands so deep in his pockets, she was afraid he would accidently push them down. The crazy thought almost had her giggling out loud, but she managed to keep it as just a smile on the outside.

That's it! That's what they're called, braces! Or is it garters, but no, garters are what women wear. Oh, whatever, she thought. That was the least of her worries right now.

'Would you like something to eat, Miss? You must be hungry by now,' Henry asked.

He was right, it must have been a while since she last ate as she could now feel her stomach rumbling. She tried to squeeze her abdomen muscles to stop the noise but wasn't quite successful, it was practically screaming FEED ME.

But if Henry heard, he certainly didn't show it.

'I don't suppose you have McDonald's?' she asked raising her eyebrows in question, although she already knew the answer.

'I don't know what that is, Miss.'

'Course you don't,' she said in a whisper, huffing.

'What was that, Miss?'

'Anything you have will be fine, thank you,' she said louder.

Giving her a nod, 'I will be back shortly.' And then quickly left the room.

All alone now, she blew out a big breath. What the hell is going on? she thought, and not for the first time, tilting her head from side to side and giving her neck a gentle squeeze to relieve some of the pain. Everything felt so tight and painful.

Was it even possible what the doctor had said? It would certainly explain a few things, the room, the clothes, the people, ok, granted she had only met three people but still, all this was creepy as hell.

If it was true and she did somehow time travel when she got hit, what now? How could she go back? Could she ever go back? she wondered. That was a very worrying question.

She had watched quite a few time travel movies, including the classic Back to the Future, all three movies in fact and they all involved some sort of time machine. But she got hit by lightning for crying out loud!

Again, her mind went back to what she could remember from school, remembering her science teacher saying that if something was to move faster than the speed of light then it would move back in time but again, nothing could move faster than the speed of light. It just wasn't possible for anything, never mind a human body, the technology just didn't exist and probably never would.

Although, there was still the possibility that this was all a joke, a stupid, sick joke. Well, she would soon find out if it was true or not.

Once she went out, she would know. There was practically a Costa coffee on every corner, not to mention all the cars and scooters everywhere.

Just then the door opened and in walked Henry with a tray.

Setting it down on the little bedside table, she saw it had a small teapot and cup complete with its saucer. Very fancy, she thought to herself. There were also sandwiches on a plate, the tiniest she had ever seen, with the crusts removed and cut into squares, there were also two hard boiled eggs, some cheese, which looked like cheddar and a couple of biscuits.

'I didn't know what you would like, so I got a bit of everything,' he said, seeing her eyeing up the contents.

'This is great, thank you.'

'I wanted to get a couple of muffins, but they were all gone.'

'It's fine honestly, thank you. I'm not even going to eat all of this,' she said.

'But where's your cup, you're not joining me?' she asked, picking up the little flowery teapot and filling up her cup.

The look on his face was one she couldn't understand, was it surprise? But why would her question surprise him?

'I thought you might wish to dine alone, Miss.'

Dine? Miss? Okay, time for a little chat, she thought to herself, taking a sip of her tea.

Clearing her throat first, 'Erm ok, first stop calling me Miss and second, dine? Seriously, who says that? And thirdly, sit and join me, you silly goose.'

She saw his lips twitch when she called him a silly goose, like he wanted to laugh or smile but was holding it in.

'Alright Mi...'

'Emily,' she said, raising her eyebrows at him in response to him nearly calling her Miss again.

God, was this guy pre-programmed or something?

'Emily,' he said, giving her a nod of his head and pulling up the only chair in the room, bringing it back to the bed to sit down on.

Picking up the plate of sandwiches, she offered it to him.

Taking one, 'Thank you,' he said, to which she just simply smiled while taking a bite of her own cucumber sandwich.

'Mmm', looking at her half-eaten sandwich, 'Is that mint?'

'I believe so,' he replied.

'It's nice,' taking another bite.

Tilting her head to the side, he's quite hot she thought to herself while eyeing him up and down.

She must have been eyeing him much longer than she thought, because when she finally looked up, she caught him watching her with what looked like amusement on his face.

'You are very strange indeed,' he said.

'Hey buddy, this is the second time you called me strange today. I could call you a few names if I wanted to, you know,' she said, pretending to be insulted.

The only words however that came to mind were - hot, sexy, drop dead gorgeous...all along those lines.

'You gonna eat that?' she asked with her mouth full, after polishing off her plate of very tiny sandwiches.

If her mother could only see her now, she would be wagging her finger saying, "Don't talk with your mouth full." She knew she was being very un-ladylike, but she didn't care, she was starving.

Smiling, he handed the tiny little sandwich over, 'I was saving it for you.'

Really? she didn't actually expect him to hand it over to her. In a way she was kind of joking, there was plenty of other food on the tray that she could eat.

'It's ok, I was only joking with you. You can have it.'

'I have eaten earlier, before you woke. Take it,' he prompted, handing her the sandwich.

'Thank you,' she said, slowly taking it from his hand and taking a bite, unable to resist.

'Besides, the way you were eating I was worried you would eat me next.'

'Hey,' she said, and without thinking gave him a playful smack on the arm, where he in turn rubbed his arm pretending it hurt. 'Ouch.'

And they both laughed.

It seemed he had a sense of humour after all, she thought.

'Would you like to come with me later to the fields?'

'Yeah sure, what you going to do there?' she asked, picturing him with a pitchfork surrounded by straw.

'Not much today, I just have to check if the potatoes are ready to be pulled out.'

'How do you know that? They're underground right? So, you can't see them.'

'Correct. But potatoes produce flowers over ground. When they start to fade or the unopened buds drop, it means the potatoes are ready to harvest.'

'Oh, ok cool,' was all she could say.

She couldn't even keep a simple houseplant alive, they almost seemed to have an allergic reaction to her. She would simply touch one and they would die, she definitely didn't have green fingers.

There was another knock on the main door and Henry quickly got up saying he'd be back and closed the door behind him.

Not long after, he came back holding some clothes over his arm and a pair of brown boots in the other.

'That was Rose, the doctor thought it best you had some different clothes for going out,' he said.

'What do you mean by different?' she asked raising her eyebrows.

'Miss, people will talk if you go outside dressed like that.'

'Like what?' Looking down at herself. Ok, he had a point, she did have dried puke on her T-Shirt, and she didn't even want to think about the dried-up piss on her jeans.

'Yeah, you got a point there. I'm disgusting,' she admitted, she didn't even need to lift her arm to smell her armpit, just little movements and the smell would waft around.

'It's not just that, Miss, but the clothes you are wearing are very strange. People here don't wear anything like that, especially women.'

Well, he had a point yet again. If indeed this was 1874, then these clothes didn't even exist yet either.

'Ok, what have you got?' she asked, getting up to have a look.

Henry handed it all over, which seemed like a lot but once she laid everything down on the bed, she saw it was actually one outfit.

There was a long brown skirt, a white shirt with long sleeves, a black shawl, but what really caught her eye and almost had her laughing out loud, not from thinking it was funny but from sheer dismay was what she presumed to be the underwear.

There was a white vest and a corset which was fine, but what she wasn't fine with was the knickers or the lack of. Instead, in their place was a pair of long frilly looking pants that looked like they went down to her knees.

'Are those what I think they are?' she asked, pointing at them.

Clearing his throat, 'Yes Miss.'

Well, what other choice did she have? She could go commando, but she didn't like that idea considering she would be wearing a skirt.

Picking them up and holding them against her to judge the size and length.

'This is so messed up,' she said, chuckling to herself.

'Why, what do...' he trailed off, suddenly going quiet.

Turning round to face him she saw he had gone red.

'What were you going to ask?'

Although by the look of sheer embarrassment on his face she had an idea, but she found it strangely cute torturing him like this.

'It was nothing, Miss.'

'It's ok, you can ask me anything, Henry,' she said in a gentle voice trying to keep the smile at bay.

'It was nothing,' he insisted, clearing his throat.

'I bet you were wondering what women wear in my time?' she asked, and he gave a little nod.

'I would show you but I'm afraid you might have a heart attack, Henry,' she said, smiling at him over her shoulder as she went back to examining the clothes.

'There is a bowl of water on the desk with soap so you can have a wash. I will leave you to get dressed now, Miss,' he said and started to head towards the door, clearly embarrassed.

'Henry?' she said as she took off her T-shirt and stood there in her bra. 'I hate being called Miss, just call me by my name.

He gave a quick nod and practically ran out the room, making her shake her head and laugh to herself, she had never met a man like him.

But she liked him! There was just something about him, an innocence, integrity, something that men didn't seem to have anymore. Henry was the perfect example of a gentleman.

She quickly stripped down and had a quick little wash with the soap and water he provided. A shower would have been good or at least a sponge, but she did the best she could with what she had, lathering up her hands and concentrating mostly on her armpits and privates. What she would give right now for a long, hot bath with bubbles, she thought sighing.

Getting dressed wasn't as complicated as she first thought it would be. She put on the long baggy bottoms and was happy to see that the corset had the clasps on the front, turned out it was far easier then fiddling with a bra behind your back. Although she gave up on that years ago and started doing the clasps on the front and yanking it round into place.

Just as she finished putting on the other items of clothing, there was a knock on the door and the sound of Henry's voice, 'Emily, are you decent?'

'Yes Henry, you can come in now.'

Turning round and facing him, as he walked in.

Doing a little curtsy. 'What you think? Do I look good?' she asked.

'Well, you don't look like a man anymore,' he replied smiling.

'Cheeky,' she said frowning, but with a smile on her face.

'Shall we go my lady?' he asked with a grin, standing up straighter and offering his arm.

'Yes, my lord.' Well, she might as well play along and have some fun.

This was the first time she saw Henry looking comfortable and playful, it made him look different somehow, more attractive if that was even possible.

Putting her arm through his, they headed out the door.

Just outside his room on the left was a long corridor leading to what looked like from this position a kitchen. She could see a long wooden table in the middle and on the other side of that was a cast iron stove. At that very moment she saw a woman walking across the room carrying a big heavy looking pot, she was wearing very similar clothes to Rose's. She had been right about it being the kitchen, then, and that woman was probably the cook.

'This way,' Henry said, gently nudging her in the opposite direction.

On their right was a set of steps that led up towards a small landing and a door. Stepping through outside, she saw there was another set of steps that led to the ground level.

Henry's room and the kitchen she now realised, were in the basement.

Looking down, she saw the small window that was high up behind his bed.

Finally reaching the top of the steps, she froze.

Looking slowly around her but without moving her head, letting her eyes do all the work. If she didn't believe them before, she certainly did now, and if she didn't feel hopelessness before, then she certainly did now.

What was in front of her was a whole different world!

'Are you ok?' he asked gently.

'Erm...' That was all she could manage to get out, what could she say? If she said 'yes' then that would have been a lie and if she told the truth, that 'no she wasn't ok, not at all,' what would that achieve? Would it magically make everything better again, would it take her back to the 21st century? No, she didn't think so.

But it felt so strange standing here looking around, not just because of the obvious time change but because she recognised the place.

In her time this place was known as the Town Hall, fair enough everything looked different but still strangely the same.

Right across from the house was the town church with the separate smaller building next to it, which used to be a school, which she now realised in this time was very much in use, seeing all the children stepping out and going on their way.

And in front of the church, just outside its gates was a well, with actual water inside as she saw both women and children lifting up buckets full.

A little way down from the school was a tall building was a sign that read 'Colman and Colman undertakers', now that definitely wasn't there in her time. Made sense though being next to a church, she thought.

On her side of the street a little way down on her right was another building she recognised very well.

'What's that building over there?' she asked Henry while pointing.

'That's the local police post,' he said.

'Well, I'll be damned,' she whispered. If she hadn't just seen a man walking out dressed like an officer, she might not have believed him.

Seeing her staring at the building almost mesmerised by it, he asked, 'Why, do you know it?' making her laugh.

'Oh, I know it alright, but it's not a police post in my time,' she said, still laughing and shaking her head in disbelief.

'What is it?' he asked.

'Well Henry,' she said pulling in her lips, 'when I was a little girl, it used to be toilets, which were always used by drug addicts and prostitutes, nowadays it's a pub. So not much has changed there really, it's still used by crack heads and hookers.' She said shrugging, thinking back to her local pub.

Turning back to face him and seeing the look of pure horror on his face had her laughing out loud.

'And the church… is that?'

'Don't worry your pretty little head, Henry, the church is ok. It's actually the only thing I can see that is still open and working in my time, the school building is still there,' pointing at the school. 'But it just sits there empty now.'

'Why? Do children not go to school in your time?'

'No, they do. We just have bigger schools now and more of them.'

'Why would you need bigger schools?'

'Well, let me ask you a question. How many children go to that school Henry?'

'I do not know, maybe ten or fifteen,' he answered.

'In my time there's a lot more people. In a single school there can be anywhere between twelve and thirty classes depending on the size of the school, and each class usually has around twenty-five to thirty children each,' she explained.

'Do all children go to school?'

'Hell yeah, it's a legal requirement. Nowadays, if a kid decides to bunk off school their parents will get a fine.'

'I think it's something like sixty pounds for each parent, or something silly like that, I'm not too sure,' she said thinking out loud.

'What?' Henry said, a little too loudly so that people walking past, turned and looked,speaking much quieter now and leaning closer like he was about to tell a secret.

'But you could buy a house with that,' he whispered.

Now this made her laugh out loud, drawing more attention their way. 'I wish! Times have definitely changed Henry,' she said, looking around.

'And I'm not sure if it was for the better or worse,' drawing in a deep breath.

It felt so overwhelming looking around and seeing everything so different yet still the same.

Technically she was still home, just at a different time. This thought brought new tears to her eyes. She quickly blinked them back and turned to find Henry watching her.

'You ok, Miss?'

'Yes Henry. Lead the way, Sir,' she said with a smile after taking a deep breath.

Chapter 5

Standing now in the "fields" as Henry called it, she was surprised to find that it was in fact the same park that was behind Stacy's house. The same but yet strangely different, just like the town they had left behind.

Looking around it now, she was sad to see it was almost bare, it didn't have the character it did in her time. Where was the majestic willow tree that she loved so much? And the pond with all the ducks she liked to feed? It was all gone!

And in its place was rows upon rows of crops.

She recognised the corn and spinach, but she didn't know what those little white flowers were that took up a lot of the space.

'What are those white flowers over there?' she asked, pointing at the countless rows in front of them.

'Those are the potatoes, all ready to dig up,' he said, rubbing his hands together eagerly.

'I never knew potatoes made flowers, until you told me earlier.'

She wasn't stupid, she knew potatoes grew in the ground and had to be dug up, but she wasn't an expert either, and this was the first time she learned that potatoes grew flowers.

'Of course, like most things. Did you not know that?' he asked.

'Me? Yeah, 'course I did,' she said, looking away hoping he wouldn't be able to tell that she was lying. Who you kidding, she thought to herself, of course he knows, you're a terrible liar, always had been.

'Where do you get yours from?' he asked.

'What? The potatoes?' she asked, seeing him nod. 'The supermarket.'

'Everything comes from the supermarket nowadays, Henry,' she said and laughed.

'You want to hear something funny?' she asked.

'Always.'

'If you ask a kid in my time where milk comes from, seven out of ten would say the supermarket,' she said and laughed louder when she saw him raise his eyebrows in disbelief.

'But milk comes from cows,' he said.

'I know.'

'And goats,' he continued.

'I know.'

'Anyway, would you like some help?' she asked.

'If you do not mind, Miss,' he said.

'I wouldn't have offered if I did. Come on, let's get this over with,' she said, clapping her own hands together.

And that's how they spent the next couple of hours, Henry digging around the plants and Emily pulling them out and dropping them in a wooden box, which Henry explained was going to be picked up this evening and taken into town, ready to be sold in the morning.

Once they finished, they sat down on the grass to take a much-needed break before walking back to town. Thank God it wasn't far, and she was already used to the walk, from walking here often in her time.

It was home but yet it wasn't, she thought to herself again.

'Are you alright Miss?' Henry asked, after she had been quiet for a while.

Turning round to face him and seeing his kind face full of concern, something in her finally broke.

'No, no, I don't think that I am, Henry,' she said and burst into tears, covering her face with her hands.

She felt his arm go around her shoulders and pull her gently into his side, where he then wrapped his other arm round her too and held her tight.

She just felt so helpless and hopeless, she just wanted to go home, but how?

She was becoming very aware of the fact that she might never go back, it wasn't as if she could just hop on a bus and go home, because there were no bloody buses!

And even if there were, they couldn't just drive you into the future. She could just hear it now, "Next stop, London 2022".

If she wasn't already crying, she would have probably been screaming like a lunatic.

To just think of everything she took for granted, in her time, and not just her but everyone, and here they had nothing. No proper transport, no phones, no internet, no McDonald's. God, what she wouldn't do for a big Mac right about now, as she felt her stomach painfully rumble for the second time that day.

She was so used to picking up the phone, day or night and ordering anything she wanted - Indian, Chinese, Burgers - anything you fancied, at the end of your fingertips. And yet they still found things to moan about she thought, remembering the time their pizza was late by ten minutes, and Craig went mad at the delivery guy and refused to pay him. These people didn't have the luxury of getting anything late, they had to make it themselves.

She didn't know how long they had been locked in this position or even how long she had been crying, but Henry was obviously a very patient man.

Bless him, she thought. He just held her tight against him with his chin resting on the top of her head, stroking her long hair at the same time, trying to soothe her.

She decided it was time to pull back when she came to the horrible realisation that she had not only wet his shirt with her tears but also with her snot, as she had both running down her face.

Discreetly wiping her nose and mouth with the back of her hand and sleeve, she slowly pulled away, looking down at her hands, not wanting him to see her face. Because let's face it, no matter who you were or how drop dead gorgeous you were, we all had two ugly faces strictly reserved for crying and sex.

'Hey Emily, look at me,' Henry said, leaning slightly forward to try and get a look at her.

'You finally called me by my name,' she said smiling, wiping away her tears and turning to look at him.

'I guess I did,' he said, in what looked like wonderment before quickly turning back to his old ways and saying, 'I do apologise if I offended, Miss...'

Before he said anything more, she quickly put him out of his misery by putting a finger to his lips and saying, 'Shhh... its ok Henry. In my time it's rude not to call a woman by her name and we definitely don't like to be called Miss.' Removing her finger and instantly seeing him relax.

Now, as for the reason why he instantly went stiff the moment she placed her finger on his lips was anyone's guess, or did she say something wrong? She wondered. Because it didn't go unnoticed how he instantly tensed up the second her finger found his lips and she could have sworn that he stopped breathing until she removed it.

They both sat there in silence for a while, just looking out at the field, the crops, the sky, each in their own thoughts. But it was a comfortable silence and she had never had that with a man before and certainly not one she had just met.

Turning her head slightly but not too much because she didn't want to make it obvious that she was checking him out.

He was actually very attractive, even with the way he was sitting with his legs drawn up and resting his arms on his knees while playing with some straw, she could see that he had long, strong looking legs.

Moving up, she saw he had his shirt sleeves rolled up to just under his elbows and again, she could see that he had strong, muscled forearms and tanned too. Working her way slowly up, she could see that his upper arms weren't short of strength either, the muscles there weren't quite straining his shirt but were there none the less. This was a man who was used to hard work and a lot of it was done outdoors, he certainly didn't get this way from going to a gym.

Looking up at his face, she was startled to see that he was watching her.

Oh god, she thought, he must think she was a complete weirdo.

So, with nothing to say, she just smiled and went back to looking straight ahead. What could she say? Sorry I was checking you out, but I can't help myself because I think you're sexy as hell, no she didn't think so.

She couldn't see that going down very well. She didn't know much about this time, but she was pretty sure women didn't say things like that to men they didn't know, probably not even to their own husbands.

'What's it like in your time?' Henry asked, surprising her.

'My time is very different Henry,' she said with a deep sigh and lying back against the grass, looking up at the sky, which for the first time was so clear and without the zigzag lines left behind by the many planes carrying people to tropical places.

She felt him lie down beside her on the grass and turned her head to face him.

'I don't even know where to begin to be honest,' looking back at the sky and resting her hands on her tummy.

'We have cars,' she said after a while. 'They can go a hundred and twenty miles an hour...'

'Is that fast?' he asked.

'Hell yeah. And some can go even faster, like racing cars.'

'What are they?'

'Still cars but are built specifically for racing, very dangerous in my opinion but some people like that kind of thing.'

'Doesn't sound very safe.'

'Trust me it's not. Let me see, what else...' she said, thinking about what else she could tell him. It was so strange, there were so many changes and differences between the times but when you had to pick them out, it was surprisingly hard to do.

'We also have planes that take people to different countries, and not just people but animals too.'

'How do they take you there?'

'They fly.' And laughed when seeing his expression.

'Wont they fall?' he asked.

'It's perfectly safe. I've been on a plane loads of times, I don't much like the take-off, it makes my stomach feel like it's dancing around. But it's not too bad and it's so worth it when you finally land in a beautiful hot country. There have been some plane crashes though,' she added. 'But statistically, your chances of being in a plane crash are one in eleven million and your chances of being struck by lightning is one in three thousand. Can you believe that! You're actually safer in a plane in the sky than walking in your local park, in the middle of a storm, with your feet firmly on the ground,' she said, shaking her own head in disbelief.

'And trust me I googled that before getting on my first plane. I was kind of scared of flying at the time,' she said, shrugging her shoulders.

'Goggle? What's that?' He asked.

'Oh yeah, how could I forget,' she said, smacking herself on the forehead, making Henry draw his eyebrows together, probably thinking she was completely and utterly bonkers.

'We have computers now and the internet. Google is just a search engine, anything you want to know, you can ask it and it has all the answers.'

'You talk to it?'

'Oh no, you just type it in and then read the answer. But Siri you can speak to, and it would actually speak back.'

'Who is that?'

'Not a who, but a what! Siri is a computer programme. I know, cool right?' she said seeing his eyes grow wide. 'She's a virtual assistant, you can ask her anything from the weather, the news or to call someone for you, literally anything. And you can have full blown conversations with her too.' Giggling now like a child, 'I once said "I love you" to see what she would say and guess what, she said "you are the wind beneath my wings",' laughing out loud at the memory.

'And this Siri is in a computer?' he asked.

'And on phones. Oh, and we also have Alexa.'

'Alexa?'

'Yeah, just the same as Siri but better. Alexa can even turn your lights on and off if you ask her to.'

'So, she's a woman?'

'No.'

'But you keep saying she,' he said, confused.

'I know, crazy right? Probably because they have women's names.' She shrugged.

'Oh, we also have the underground...'

'Underground?'

She realised she was throwing names of things at him that he had no clue what they were because they didn't even exist yet, and to top it off, she wasn't very good at explaining things either.

'Sorry, I'm not good at explaining things, I'm probably confusing you even more,' she said.

'Right, how do I explain this?' She thought out loud.

'Ok, we have these things called trains. They carry people like cars, but unlike a car which can only carry between five to seven people, a train can carry much more. They go very fast, faster than a racing car and they travel through a series of underground tunnels.'

Using her hands to try and explain it by making a circle with her thumb and finger with one hand and poking a finger through it with her other, before realising what she was doing and the double meaning of it.

Going bright red, she put her hands back down.

'Anyway, they take you anywhere in London, faster than a car.'

'Why would you go underground?' he asked, looking puzzled.

'Because there are so many people that we simply cannot all travel on ground. There are too many cars, buses, bikes even, and there's already too much traffic. We simply just don't fit.'

'I don't understand. You people are strange,' he said.

'This one would make your brain explode,' she said laughing.

'We also have the Eurotunnel where a train takes you to France, so no need to get on a plane,' she said looking at his face eager to see his expression. 'And that goes under the sea!' she added, raising her eyebrows and giving him a smile.

This was fun, she thought.

'You people sure do some crazy stuff, and dangerous, may I add?'

'Oh, it's not that bad. We also have McDonald's; they do these amazing huge burgers...' showing him with her hands and exaggerating with the size. 'And KFC, Chinese, Indian, Mexican food, anything you fancy, we got it,' almost salivating at the thought of all that food.

'And of course the famous Uber,' he said.

'Wh...' and when she looked at him, she saw him smiling and realised he was making fun of himself for thinking it was food.

It was a sweet smile, one that made her want to reach out and touch his cheek. But instead, she smiled and said, 'And of course the famous Uber.' Making them both, laugh.

They both fell back into that comfortable silence again as they both looked up at the sky, which was now beginning to turn into shades of orange and pink.

It was beautiful.

She had never got the chance to fully enjoy the sunset before; she was either on a bus, working or at home watching crap on the telly. If she ever made it back home, she swore she would make the effort to at least look at the sunset from her window.

'We should head back soon before it gets dark,' Henry said, just as a breeze picked up. 'And before it gets too cold, the temperature drops quite low in the evening.'

'Ok.'

As they both sat up, another breeze swept a small branch against her leg. About to brush it away, she instantly recognised the shape of the very few little leaves that were on the stick.

Getting overly excited, like seeing an old friend, she turned to him and practically squeaked, 'Henry, this is from a willow tree.'

'Looks like you might be right, but we don't have any willow trees around here, it must have been dropped by a bird,' he said, pulling back slightly because she practically stuck the twig in his face.

And seeing the look of excitement in her eyes for the first time, he had this overwhelming need to keep that look on her face. Standing up he reached down and took her hand, pulling her up with him.

'Let's plant it,' he said.

'What, really? We can do that?'

'Of course.'

'I mean, will it work, will it grow? Is what I'm trying to say, just planting a stick in the ground.'

'Of course. You have more chance of something to grow if you plant a branch of it, rather than a seed.'

Looking around she realised for the first time, that they had been sitting in exactly the same spot where the willow tree was in her time! And she knew in that moment, without a shadow of a doubt, that what they were about to plant would grow and flourish.

'Where should we plant it?' he asked, looking around.

'Here,' she said, looking up at him.

'Here?'

'Yes, this very spot.'

'Alright then.'

Bending back down he began to dig a little hole with his hands and bending down she put the little twig in and helped him put the soil back in place.

'Here, pour some water on to it,' he said, handing her a bottle that was bound in leather.

Reaching out to take the water, she felt an electric shock the instant their fingers touched. Pulling back instantly she said, 'Did you feel that?'

'Yes, I did. What was that?'

'I think it was a sign, that this branch was meant to be planted,' she said, looking up at him and smiling.

'How do you know?' he asked, looking at her with narrowed eyes. She was a very strange woman indeed, he thought.

'Because Henry, we already did.'

She was one strange lady, maybe it was that bang to her head, he thought.

He would have remembered a simple act as planting a branch; besides he had only just met her, and she had been passed out in his room until this afternoon.

'Erm… Miss…'

'Oh, don't worry Henry,' she said, laughing out loud.

'I haven't lost my marbles or anything. Not yet anyway.' And seeing the confused and worried look on his face, decided to put the poor man out of his misery. Well, she didn't want him thinking she was crazy, or crazier, as she was pretty sure that he already thought she was kind of a nut job.

'I'll explain. You see, in my time, this...' she said looking around her, 'is my local park. Over there is a massive man-made pond.' Pointing towards the potato crops.

'It has ducks and beautiful white swans which I come and feed often or used to. And here, this very spot we are standing on...' pointing down at their feet, 'is my favourite willow tree. I always come to it when I feel sad or down, it feels like having an angel's wings wrapped around me... it feels like home,' she said, blinking back the tears that she could feel building up and choking her. 'So, you see Henry...' taking his hands in hers and holding them tight, 'I just know that this is the tree,' she said, feeling the tears stinging the back of her throat.

It was a strange feeling seeing that branch and realising where they had been sitting, she felt comforted, like she was no longer alone.

Looking at her now, she was so certain of what she was saying and who knew maybe she was right. There was a lot going on that he didn't understand but one thing he was certain of, and that was that she needed this. She needed this to be true and who was he to destroy that hope he saw in her eyes this very moment.

Wiping away the single tear that travelled down her cheek with his thumb, 'Let's water our tree,' he said.

After watering "their tree" as Henry called it, they slowly made their way back and it was lucky that they left when they did, because the second they entered the town, it started to pour down with rain.

Running towards the house, she was thankful that she had been holding on to Henry and that he was as strong as he looked, because she slipped a couple of times and nearly went down, almost taking him with her. The roads seemed so slippery or maybe it was just the boots she was wearing, well, the right one definitely had a hole or two in it as it felt like she had a puddle in it. A very cold puddle.

By the time they entered the house and went to Henry's room, she was soaked through.

She was happy, over the moon, in fact to see that there was another outfit laid out on the bed for her.

Running over and picking them up, 'Yes, yes, yes, dry clothes.'

'Rose must have bought them round for you. Let's get you dry before you catch your death,' he said, going over to the wardrobe and getting out a towel.

Coming over to her, he raised the towel towards her and for a moment there it seemed like he was about to dry her hair, before he pulled back and handed her the towel.

'Sorry,' he said quietly, looking down.

'That's ok,' she said, taking the towel from him.

That was such an awkward and unexpected moment, but one that strangely made her heart jump in her chest.

Did she want him to dry her hair? It wasn't the drying process, it was the intimacy of the act. Did she want that with Henry?

She didn't even know the guy!

He seemed like a nice guy, but it was only this morning that she thought he was a kidnapper, and let's be honest, she didn't exactly have a good track record when it came to men. Just look at her last relationship, an absolute train crash!

'I'll leave you to get changed, I'll be back with some dinner soon.'

Seeing him heading towards the door, she stopped him.

'Erm, Henry...'

'Yes?' he asked, looking back.

'I would really like to wash my own clothes and I'm guessing you don't have a washing machine.'

'I'll bring in some water. I'll be back in a minute.'

And sure enough, he was back with a big bucket of water and a bar of soap.

'So that's how you wash your clothes.'

'Of course, Miss.'

'Of course it is,' she said, nodding her head and smiling, partly because it didn't go unnoticed that he was back to calling her Miss again.

'So, do I just soap it up and...rub?' she asked.

She never thought she would ever say a sentence like that!

She should have just kept her mouth shut and got on with it, what must this man think of her!

'Yes, Miss... Have you never... done this before?' he asked slowly.

Oh god, she wanted to hide her face in shame. She felt like a complete idiot, and she didn't want him thinking she was one.

'Well, we don't have to wash by hand in the 21st century, Henry. We have washing machines now, you know.'

'My apologies, Miss, I didn't mean to offend you.'

Oh god, she didn't realise how bitchy that was going to sound until she said it. Maybe she should take her mother's advice and think before she speaks.

'No Henry, you didn't offend me. I'm so sorry, I didn't mean it to come out that way.'

She really was an idiot!

'Please forgive me,' she added.

'Would you like me to help...'

'God no! I mean, that's very kind of you but I'm sure I'll manage. Thank you.'

'Ok, I'll leave you to it.'

Seeing him close the door behind him, she let out a breath that she didn't realise she had been holding in and suddenly shivered.

Jesus, but it was freezing.

Quickly stripping out of the wet clothes, she used the towel to wipe herself dry before quickly getting dressed in the dry clothes Rose had left for her on the bed.

She really missed her comfy jogging bottoms and jumpers, these clothes were really uncomfortable and the corset was making her boobs itchy, probably because they were so squashed together.

Looking around, she found a hanger on the handle of the wardrobe door and hung up the soaking dress to dry.

Going over to the bucket, she washed her underwear, t-shirt and jeans with the bar of soap and water and laid them over the back of the chair to dry.

Looking down at them, she put her hands on her hips and smiled. She done a pretty decent job, at least they didn't stink of piss anymore, she thought to herself.

Just as she was stepping back, the door suddenly opened and thinking it was Henry she looked up and smiled, only to see a woman in the most amazing pale pink dress standing just inside the door, staring at her.

'Erm… are you looking for Henry?' she asked.

'Considering this is his room, yes I am,' she replied in a rather sharp tone.

Ok, she didn't like this woman, straight out.

'Henry's not here at the moment,' she said, staring back at her. She wasn't about to let this woman intimidate her.

'I can see that,' she said, wrinkling her nose while looking around the room.

'Well, he should be back soon…'

'I sure hope so, and what are you doing in this room? Does Henry know you are here?'

Oh, she REALLY didn't like this woman.

'Yes, he does. And haven't you heard of knocking?' she asked, folding her arms across her chest.

'My word, how rude. I will have you know that this is my house, and I can enter any room I wish.'

'Rude? Oh, you haven't seen rude yet…'

Just then Henry came back carrying two steaming bowls on a tray.

'Henry, you know the rules about having her kind under this roof,' she said this while looking her up and down, like she was the shit on her shoe.

'And what is that supposed to mean?' she asked. Who the hell did this woman think she is treating people like this?

'This is my sister, My Lady,' Henry quickly replied, after putting down the tray and coming to stand between them.

'My Lady? Oh, you have got to be shitting me.' This woman was anything but a lady!

'You never mentioned you had a sister before.' she said, looking at Henry and ignoring Emily.

'I'm sorry, My Lady,' Henry said, standing tall and with his hands behind his back.

Looking down she saw he was wringing his hands behind his back, it was obvious this woman made him nervous.

'Will she be staying here long?'

'Just a couple of weeks, My Lady, she's visiting me from up north.'

'I see... I shall leave you to your meal.'

Seeming satisfied, she turned to leave. Just before closing the door behind her, she turned back round. 'Oh, and Henry... when you get the chance can you pop upstairs? I have something that needs fixing.'

'Yes, My Lady,' he said, nodding.

And with that she left, closing the door behind her.

'Bitch.' She couldn't help it, it just came out of her mouth.

'We should eat while it's still hot,' he said, pointing towards the tray.

'I saw that, you know,' she said, smiling at him.

'You saw what?' he asked, heading over to the desk where the tray of food was.

'I saw you smile when I called her a bitch,' she said, following him.

Taking her bowl, she went back towards the bed, where she sat crossed legged with the bowl on her lap.

Seeing her clothes on the back of the chair, he took his bowl and went to join her by sitting on the end of the bed

'Who was she anyway?' she had a slight inkling but couldn't be sure.

'She's my boss.'

'I thought so. That explains it then.' So, she had been right.

'Explains what?'

'Her bitchiness!' she replied, taking a spoonful of what looked and smelled like beef stew.

'Oh my god, this is so amazing,' she said with her mouth still full, making Henry laugh.

'You've never had stew before?'

'Of course I have, but not like this. You can actually taste all the different flavours, unlike the tasteless stuff we have back home.'

'I don't understand, why is it tasteless?' he asked, while enjoying his own.

'Well, this is obviously organic, isn't it? The vegetables in this bowl have been grown and picked in the fields...'

'Of course, where else?'

'The food we have in my time is mostly made from chemicals, that's why they are tasteless. And the organic stuff is so expensive, not a lot of people can afford it.'

'How are they made from chemicals? I don't understand,' frowning, he really didn't understand half the things this woman said. Her time sounded so complicated and crazy, thinking back to what she told him about flying machines and travelling underground like moles.

'When I say chemicals, what I mean is that they spray them with chemicals to keep all the bugs away and help them grow bigger. But they are actually very bad for our health, not to mention the fruit and vegetables don't taste like they should. And don't even get me started on the chicken.'

'Why? What do they do to the chickens?'

'They literally inject them with chemicals and hormones to make them bigger so they can slaughter them and sell them quicker. I once saw something on YouTube, where they injected a chicken leg with something, and you could see it swell up to double its size. Then they just packaged it up and off to the supermarket shelves it went. Then we poor sods buy it and end up dying from cancer.'

'Why would you eat that?' he asked, looking disgusted by what he just heard.

'What else can we eat? It's everywhere, and like I said, the organic stuff is very expensive, and the only decent priced things are the things that are bad for you.'

'But why? It's almost as if they want you dead.'

'Exactly Henry, now you're getting it,' she said, while stuffing another spoonful in her mouth.

'Getting what?' he asked, looking puzzled.

Looking up at him, she had an overwhelming need to suddenly pinch his cheeks.

'How's yours?' she asked, pointing towards his own bowl, changing the subject.

'Yes, it's good,' he said, continuing to eat and she could have sworn she heard him mumbling something about it being made in the same pot.

They settled into a comfortable silence while they ate, until Henry suddenly asked,

'What's YouTube?'

Smiling up at him, 'It's an internet thing. You can watch videos and upload your own as well.'

Watching him nod his head in thought then go back to his meal.

'Sorry, Henry, if I'm not explaining things properly. I've never had to explain this sort of stuff before.'

She felt bad for not explaining things properly, but it was hard, everybody in her time just grew up with all those things, they didn't need explaining.

'It's ok, I understand. You're doing a good job.'

Once they finished their meal, Henry took their bowls back to the tray and asked if she wanted seconds. She desperately wanted to say yes as that stew was the best she had ever had, but she didn't want to seem like a pig, so ended up reluctantly saying no instead.

One thing she noticed since waking up here, was that the women all seemed smaller, thinner than in her time.

She had only had lunch and dinner here so far but if all the portions were so ridiculously tiny then no wonder, remembering the tiny little sandwiches she had for lunch.

After taking the bowls back to the kitchen, Henry came back with two plates of what looked like Victoria sponge slices, and she was happy to see he gave her the biggest slice.

'Oh wow, cake, thank you,' she said, almost salivating.

And it was almost embarrassing to see that she polished off her plate before Henry.

They spent quite some time after just sitting on the bed and talking, mostly with Henry asking questions about the future, and her doing her best to answer them as simply and as best she could. But every answer she gave prompted another question from Henry.

But she didn't mind, it was actually really nice, and she was surprised to find that she was really enjoying herself.

They spent so much time on the TV, computers and mostly phones in her time, that they didn't enjoy the simple pleasures of just talking with each other anymore.

Something she had to admit she was also guilty of.

Finally, they both ended up yawning, and that's when it started to get quite awkward.

'Erm... how do we go about this? I can sleep on the floor, I really don't mind...'

'No, Miss, I won't hear of it. You're a lady, you cannot sleep on the floor like an animal.'

She smiled at being called a lady, she had never been called that before. It was sweet.

'You take the bed, Miss, I will sleep on the chair.'

Walking over to the said chair by his desk, was the moment when she wanted to laugh out loud, but somehow had managed to hold it in. Now, how she managed to hold it in, she had no idea, as the look on Henry's face when he encountered her thong on the chair was priceless.

He picked it up and started looking at it, turning it around in his hands.

'What is this, Miss?'

Barely holding it together, she replied, 'It's a thong.' Purposefully not explaining what it was, knowing he was going to ask.

'What do you do with it?'

'You wear it,' she said, grinning now.

'I see.' Nodding his head, and turning it around and upside down, obviously trying to figure out where.

If he tried putting it on his head, she would just faint from laughing so hard.

'Where?'

'Where what?' Oh, but she was being mean, and she knew it.

'Where do you wear it, Miss?' he asked, turning round to face her now.

This was the moment she could no longer hold it in and burst out laughing. She tried to speak but couldn't get the words out of her mouth, because every time she tried to say the words, she would end up laughing even harder. She was crying from it and her stomach ached at the sight of Henry laughing just as hard, while holding her thong.

Once she calmed down a bit which took a while, she managed to inform him that it was actually underwear.

Getting up and taking the thong from him, she put it against herself to show him.

'But where's the back bit?'

'It's here.' Showing him the stringy bit at the back.

'It goes up your bum,' she informed him, laughing again at his wide eyes.

'Doesn't it hurt? Why would you do that to yourself?'

'It's actually very comfortable, you don't even feel it. Way more comfortable than the stuff you wear here, I can tell you.'

'Your time is very strange.'

Adding quietly, 'And the women are stranger,' as he turned towards the wardrobe to get some hangers.

'I heard that!'

'Well, it's true, Miss. You say it's comfortable, but I can't imagine it to be.'

'Men wear them too you know.'

'Now you must be making fun of me.'

'No, it's true, seriously.'

'But where would their... never mind,' giving his head a shake.

She knew exactly what the poor guy was thinking, which was why she said, 'You can try them on if you want. You know, just to see how they fit,' giving him a wink and then laughing when he suddenly went red.

She had to stop torturing the poor man.

'I'm only joking but let me know if you change your mind.'

'I can assure you I will not.'

Giving her some hangers, she hung up her clothes to dry and to free up the chair which he insisted on sleeping on.

Giving her one of his shirts to wear to bed, he left the room to allow her to get changed. He was such a gentleman; men like him didn't exist in her time.

By the time he came back wearing his own pj's, she was already changed and getting under the covers.

'You know Henry, this bed is small, but I think it can fit the both of us.'

'No, Miss, it's not proper for a lady to share a bed with a man who isn't her husband.'

Ok, this was sweet but also getting ridiculous, he was beginning to sound like her grandmother.

'Henry, I'm no lady, trust me on that. And in my time, it's not uncommon for a man and a woman to share a bed. People very rarely get married in my time. So, it's ok, and besides we don't know how long I'm going to be stuck here for and you can't sleep on that bloody chair.'

'But...'

'No but's Henry. It's ok, nobody will know.'

Finally persuading him, he slowly climbed into the bed as if he was still mentally battling against his decision and his morals.

Once he was under the covers, he turned on his side, so he was facing away from her.

'Goodnight, Henry,' she said.

'Goodnight, Miss.'

Chapter 6

Waking up the next morning, she almost forgot where she was and for a split-second thought she was back home in her own bed, that was until she heard Henry speak.

'Good morning, Miss.'

And just like that she was back in the present.

'Good morning, Henry.'

Taking a longer look at him, she saw he was fully clothed and looking very tired if those bags under his eyes were anything to go by.

'Did you manage to get any sleep?' she asked.

'Yes, Miss.'

Yeah right, she thought.

'I believe you, thousands wouldn't,' she said.

'I bought you some breakfast,' taking a tray over to her and placing it on her lap.

There was a pot of tea, six slices of toast, marmalade, honey, butter, two hard boiled eggs and some fresh fruit.

Her face must have really lit up at the sight of all the food, because Henry started to laugh and said, 'I knew you had a big appetite, so I made more toast.'

Making her feel like a proper pig, but a very happy pig. So, she just snorted at him and stuck her tongue out.

Spreading butter and honey on her toast, she noticed him putting his boots on.

'Are you not joining me?' she asked with her mouth full. She really needed to remember her table manners, she thought.

'No Miss, I have already eaten.'

'Bloody hell, what time do you get up?'

'Very early Miss. I have some errands to run and will be out for most of the day, but Rose will come by soon to keep you company. If there's anything you need just let her know.'

'Ok.'

Giving her a nod, he put on his hat, which she could only describe as a golfer's hat and headed towards the door.

Sitting there alone she finished her breakfast, and got dressed, only this time wearing her own underwear. That corset was so uncomfortable and hard she wondered how the women here coped with wearing them on a daily basis.

Thank God for the bra invention!

Sitting there now all alone with nothing to do, she suddenly became very homesick again and found herself crying. It was ok when Henry was here because he kept her distracted and she liked his company. She laughed more in one day with Henry then she had the last year with Craig.

Maybe she should go for a walk she thought. She knew the area, so it wasn't like she was going to get lost or anything. But then she remembered Henry saying that Rose was going to pop by, so she decided to stay and wait, she didn't want to seem rude or ungrateful, especially when she was wearing the girl's clothes.

Surprisingly she didn't have to wait long, as soon after there was a knock on the door and a soft voice say, 'It's me Miss, Rose.'

Recognising her voice, she instantly jumped up and opened the door, surprising Rose in the process by giving her a huge hug like they were long lost friends.

She didn't quite know what had come over her, she was just so happy to see a familiar kind face.

When she finally let the poor girl go, she stepped back allowing Rose to step into the room, and that was when she noticed that Rose had the doctor's bag with her.

'You here to examine me?' she joked.

'No, Miss,' Rose answered shyly.

And she felt instantly bad, the poor girl probably wasn't used to jokes. And neither was Henry for that matter, people really needed to chill more, she thought to herself.

'I just meant... because you have the doctor's case that's all,' she said, pointing at the bag.

'Oh no, this is the doctor's old bag. He gave it to me to keep for myself,' she said proudly.

'Oh ok,' she said, suddenly feeling awkward as they both just stood there looking at each other.

Then Rose put the case down on the desk and opened it to produce a couple of books.

'I brought you some books, Miss,' she said, handing her the books.

Taking them, she nearly screamed out loud.

Clutching them to her chest she gasped, 'Wuthering Heights.'

'OMG, this is my favourite book of all time, well, apart from Pride and Prejudice.'

Turning over the other book and seeing the title, "North and South", another of her favourites. She walked up to Rose and gave her another big hug.

'Thank you.' Was all she could say, while feeling a lump rise in her throat and tears stinging her eyes.

'It's my pleasure, Miss. The doctor said to bring them over.'

This meant so much to her, it was actually a life saver.

She loved books, all books, she was never one to stick to just one genre like most people did, although she did have her favourites.

Back home she had three huge bookcases full of books and back when she was a teen and her book obsession began, she went as far as keeping a list of all the books she had, including who they were written by, a proper inventory. She must have been a librarian in her past life.

And she had never lent any of her books out to anybody apart from Stacy, and that was because they had the same obsession with books, so she knew they were in safe hands.

She hated the way some people folded books back when reading, causing crease lines along the spine, it gave her the shivers.

Craig never understood her love for the written word, had always taken the piss out of her and would tell her to get a life.

One time he got home drunk and had the fucking cheek to rip off a small corner of a book she had on the coffee table to use as a filter on his roll-ups. God, it made her blood boil just thinking about that day!

'Thank you Rose. This means so much to me, I love reading,' she said, clutching the books close to her heart.

'So, you know how to read then, Miss?' Rose asked.

'Of course, who doesn't,' she answered all too quickly without thinking. As soon as the words were out of her mouth, she instantly regretted saying them.

Seeing Rose just smile timidly and look down at her shoes, she knew that the girl couldn't read, it was clear as day.

'Oh, Rose, I'm so sorry. I didn't realise.'

'It's ok, Miss.'

'No, it's not ok. I always speak without thinking first and it's wrong.'

'It's ok, Miss. The doctor did try teaching me a couple of years ago but...' shrugging her shoulders. 'I guess I'm not smart enough.'

'Don't be so silly. Who said you're not smart enough?' shocked to hear her speaking like that about herself.

'Nobody Miss, it's just me thinking, is all.'

'Well, you're silly. I bet I can teach you.'

'Really, Miss?'

Seeing her eyes light up for the first time since meeting her, she resolved there and then that she wouldn't give up until she taught Rose how to read and write.

'Sure, it'll be fun, I promise,' she said with a smile.

'But what if I don't understand?' she said, suddenly looking worried.

'You will. With my way you will. Can you get me some paper and pen?'

'Yes Miss, tomorrow when I come by, I'll bring some with me.'

'Good, then your first lesson begins tomorrow.'

As well as the books, Rose also brought her a cross stitch pattern to do. Apparently it was going to be turned into a pillowcase.

Rose spent what felt like hours patiently teaching her how to cross stitch and she surprised herself by how much she really enjoyed it. She could easily spend a day just reading and sewing.

After a while Rose suggested going for a walk in the fields to get her out of the house for a bit. So, they took a little stroll, and she surprised Rose by linking her arm through hers and they walked quietly, each in their own thoughts.

She liked Rose and really hoped they could become friends, there was just something about her that she just couldn't quite put her finger on.

After a while of walking in silence, Rose asked, 'What's it like in your time?'

Emily just looked at her, not quite sure what to say.

'The doctor explained it all to me last night, Miss, said it was probably the lightning that brought you here.'

Taking a deep breath, she said. 'Well, it's different that's for sure. What would you like to know?'

'I don't know, Miss, anything and everything,' she said.

'Ok, erm… we have TVs…'

'TVs?'

'Yes, it's like a big flat box and we watch stuff on it, like a theatre in a box,' she said, hoping she explained it well.

'Where you walk or travel by horse to get to places, we travel by cars, buses and trains. They are like… I don't know how to explain it, but they are like big machines with seats inside that you direct which way they go, just like a horse. But you don't get wet or cold.'

She hoped she had explained it well, but either way Rose looked intrigued and was watching her intently.

Finding a nice quite spot they decided to sit down, and she continued to talk more about the future.

She decided to tell Rose a bit about some of the changes that occurred in women's lives over the years. She told her about the invention of the bra and even showed her a bit of her bra strap, prompting Rose to go bright red.

She then went on to explain how women can now vote and even work in politics. She also went on to tell her how in her time being prime minster wasn't just reserved for men, but for women too.

'Women now have strong positions, some are lawyers, police officers, judges, teachers, doctors - the list is endless. Anything men can do, we can do better. There's still the issue about equal pay in some places but generally they get paid the same and some even more than men.'

'Wow!' Rose was completely stunned and staring straight ahead almost like she was picturing the future.

'Women are doctors? It's unbelievable,' she said in a whisper.

'Believe it sweetie, everything is possible in the future.'

'If I was in your time, do you think I could have become a doctor?'

'If you wanted to, you could be anything you want,' she said, smiling, 'Do you want to be a doctor, Rose?' she asked, because she got the feeling that maybe Rose had wanted more out of her life.

'Yes, but I guess being the doctor's helper is the next best thing,' she said, shrugging her shoulders and smiling. Although Emily noticed that the smile never reached her eyes.

Again, it made her think about how much people liked to moan and complain about almost everything in her time and they didn't realise how good they actually had it, how lucky they were. Her included!

They sat there for a while, both asking each other questions.

Rose told her a bit about her life, how her parents had both died when she was a teen and how the kind doctor had taken her in, taught her how to do some basic nursing, such as changing bandages and checking temperatures. And Emily had told her all about Craig and everything he had put her through.

She listened wide eyed and was very shocked to hear that women and men lived together out of marriage. But she wasn't judgemental in the least, instead she wondered why Emily had let him get away with so much.

Recounting everything again about Craig and everything he had put her through, made her feel angry all over again, but not at him this time but at herself.

'I was such a fool, Rose,' she said.

Reaching out, Rose put the back of her hand on Emily's forehead and then placed it on her cheek.

'What are you doing?' Emily asked, laughing.

'Just checking you don't have a fever, Miss. Fevers make people say crazy things and calling yourself a fool is a crazy thing indeed, Miss. He was the fool, not you.'

'Oh, Rose, thank you. That means a lot, even if you are calling me crazy,' she said.

'My pleasure, Miss,' she said with a smile and a proud look on her face. 'Besides, if you don't mind me saying, but I think you should have chopped his, you know what, off.' She added this last bit with a hand by her mouth and whispering.

Making Emily laugh out loud. 'My, my, Rose, and there I thought you were an innocent girl.'

'Or poisoned his drink.' Rose added, with Emily opening her mouth pretending to be shocked and they both laughed.

Rose had really surprised her today, making the saying "never judge a book by its cover" come to mind.

'You know, Rose, you remind me so much of someone I know.'

Looking at her now, having the kind of conversation they were having and Rose saying what she just said, she reminded her so much of Stacy. She even kind of looked like her.

'Really, Miss, who?'

'My best friend.'

True to her word, Rose turned up the next day just after noon and with her she brought a pen and some paper.

They soon settled into a routine, spending a couple of hours on learning, in which Emily introduced Rose to phonics.

First, she taught her the sounds and then they began to read, simple words to begin with like cat, dog, hat... helping her to sound them out.

They would always end the lesson walking to the fields where they would sit down, and Emily would read her a chapter or two of Wuthering Heights, which she was pleased to see that Rose had quickly become a fan of.

Most of the time Henry would meet them at the fields bringing with him some lunch, which usually consisted of sandwiches, scones and fruit.

They would all sit for what seemed like hours and eat, talk, read and laugh together.

Of course it wasn't all just play and no work as Henry also tended to the crops, and Emily soon found her eyes wandering in his direction.

On a few occasions she thought she caught him looking at her but wasn't too sure as he would quickly look away.

All this didn't go unnoticed by Rose, who would giggle.

'I think he likes you, Miss,' she said to Emily one day in a whisper, after she kept pausing in her reading because her eyes kept wandering in another direction, a direction which contained a very hot, sweaty and shirtless Henry.

'Do you really think?' she asked, trying to keep the excitement out of her voice.

'Of course, he can't stop looking over, Miss.'

'He's probably looking at you,' she said, looking down and pulling at the grass.

'Craig was always interested in everybody else apart from me,' she said, shrugging her shoulders and pretending not to care.

She was tired of getting hurt and rejected, maybe if she pretended not to care long enough then maybe one day she actually wouldn't!

'Henry isn't Craig, Miss,' Rose said gently, putting a hand over hers. 'Not all men are the same, Miss.'

Taking a deep breath and blowing it out, she said, 'You're probably right Rose, but there's no point starting anything when the end might be right around the corner.'

'What do you mean?' she asked.

'I came here so suddenly that I might end up leaving again, just as suddenly. We just don't know.'

'If I understand it right, you came here because you got struck by lightning?'

'Yeah, and?'

'Well, what are the chances that you would get struck by lightning twice?'

'Yeah, I suppose you're right.'

She was a smart cookie, this Rose, she thought. Maybe she was right and maybe there wasn't a way back and this was her home now.

'I, for one, Miss, wish you never go back. You're the first friend I ever had.'

Hearing this brought tears to her eyes, and she held on to Rose's hand.

'Oh Rose, you don't know what you mean to me. You're the one who kept me sane the past few weeks. And you know what? I think I secretly don't want to go back either.'

'Really?' Her eyes were full of excitement.

'Really. Not that I have much choice in the matter anyway. Like you said, what are the chances that I will get struck by lightning twice in my life.'

✳✳✳

That evening like every other, they walked Rose back to the doctor's house which was at the end of their street before going back to their own room.

After finishing a dinner of chicken and leek pie with buttery mash, they ended up playing a few games of noughts and crosses, which annoyingly Henry kept winning at. Not that she minded that much, although she was known for being a sour loser. When she and Stacy were kids and would play computer games, whenever it seemed like she was about to lose, she would switch off the game by the main switch so they would have no option but to begin again.

Of course Stacy always took that as a win and would call her a sour loser while doing the L sign with her finger and thumb, to which Emily would respond by sticking her tongue out and restarting the game.

'Hey, I know, let's arm wrestle,' she said.

'What?'

'It's easy, I'll show you....'

'No, I know how to arm wrestle, but are you sure? You're not exactly having a winning streak, are you? And everyone knows that men are...'

'What? Stronger than women?' she asked, raising her eyebrows and crossing her arms.

'Well... Yeah.'

'What a load of bull! Maybe the "ladies" in your time, but not me. Come on, I bet I can give you a run for your money.'

'Ok, bring it on,' he said laughing.

Henry moved the bedside table so they could both position themselves on either side.

'Right buster, I'm ready to take you down.'

She never claimed to be the strongest woman or anything, but she had always been told that she was freakishly strong.

She even beat Craig once but then again, he had been drunk at the time.

Looking back, she didn't think he was ever actually sober, wow, she really did walk around with her eyes closed, back then.

Taking hold of each other's hand in a tight grip.

'Don't cry like a girl when I beat you,' he said with a wink.

'Omg, you, cheeky sod,' she said, laughing.

'Right, on three,' she said.

'Ok, one, two, thr...'

She didn't wait for him to say three, she knew she was cheating but only slightly. It wasn't like she was tickling him or anything.

Not that it gave her any sort of advantage as it was a standstill for a few seconds, mainly because Henry was playing with her.

The woman was strong, he thought. But not that strong.

He decided to put her out of her misery because she was starting to go red, she wasn't a quitter that was for sure.

One hard push and her hand touched now.

'Got you,' he said.

'Wait, again, I wasn't ready,' she said.

'Oh, really,' he said, laughing.

'Yeah, really.'

And with both of them laughing they gripped each other's hand again.

'Ok, but you're counting this time,' he said.

'Ok. One...'

And her hand instantly went down.

'Hey... that's not fair. That's cheating.'

'You cheated first,' he stated.

'Yes... but...'

'But? I thought you said women in your time liked to be treated equally.'

'Yeah... well... we're not in my time though, are we?' she said crossing her arms and pretending to be cross.

Suddenly he leaned forward and gave her a quick kiss on the lips.

The instant he pulled back he regretted what he had done, he certainly hadn't planned it, he had reacted purely on impulse.

She didn't pull back however or push him away but then, again, the kiss hadn't been long enough.

But at least she didn't slap him after, he thought. He did however catch her slight shiver and hoped she didn't find him repulsive.

Instead, she smiled and touched his hand which was still on the table between them.

Seeing her hesitantly lean forward, he took a chance and leaned the rest of the way and when she didn't pull back, he placed his lips on hers in a slow tender kiss.

Deepening the kiss, he placed his hand beneath her ear and smoothed his thumb along her jaw, making her tremble with pleasure.

He savoured her delicious soft lips, but it wasn't enough, he wanted to taste more of her. As he gently pushed with his tongue, she instantly responded by allowing him access to delve deeper inside the warmth of her mouth, catching her moan of pleasure.

Taking the hand which was holding her in place, she pulled back, breaking off the kiss. Looking into his eyes she saw the uncertainty there, but she also saw the same level of desire that was mirrored in her own.

Letting go off his hand, she stood up and pushed the bedside table back to the side, leaving no barrier between them and started to step backwards towards the bed, hoping he would follow. A kiss was one thing but sleeping together was something else entirely, especially for Henry.

Shit! what would she do if he didn't?

But thankfully Henry followed.

✳✳✳

Lying down beside Emily in the early hours of the morning, twirling a strand of her hair around his finger, he found he couldn't stop smiling.

He wasn't experienced like most other men his age, in fact it was his first time, but last night had been amazing.

It was the most perfect, beautiful night of his life.

Thinking back to last night, the feel of her skin beneath his fingertips, the feel of her hot wet centre around him, the way she clung to him, her teeth gently scraping along his shoulder, remembering every single detail had him growing hard all over again.

A miracle had bought her to him, he wasn't quite sure how she got here but it was a miracle nonetheless. He just prayed that she would stay, that she wouldn't get ripped away from this time like she did from hers or worse that she would walk away thinking him unsuitable.

He wasn't stupid, he knew his place and knew he didn't have much to offer her, people in his position rarely did. Apart from love and loyalty and they were both hers to keep, he thought looking down at her and softly stroking her cheek while she slept.

She was everything a woman should be, beautiful, kind, caring, clever, brave and strong.

Look at how she had handled this whole situation, she must have felt so scared and alone that day, waking up to a brand-new world, a different time to her own. Even though the fear in her eyes that day was clear for him to see, she didn't show it in her attitude.

And everything she had done since, teaching Rose how to write and read, working the fields with him, making new friends, how she easily and quickly adapted to the new life around her just showed how strong she really was.

He'd never known anyone with her strength, man or woman, and for that she was the bravest woman he had ever met, and he admired her for it.

She was also very highly opinionated and spoke her mind "a lot", which many women in his time did not, he thought with a smile. But he loved that about her the most.

She was honest.

He was going to marry this woman and soon, if she would have him, of course.

He had got to know her well enough over the past couple of months, to know that he wanted to spend the rest of his life with her.

But there was just one problem with that plan, they had to leave this place!

He had introduced Emily to the lady of the house as his sister and he knew her well enough to know that she would cause them problems if the truth came out.

Not to mention that she had been trying to seduce him the past few months, even before Emily turned up.

She would randomly just open the door to his room and walk in, pretending she needed something fixed or ask some ridiculous question. And always at the same time, in the evenings after working the fields when she knew he would be back and getting changed.

Since Emily turned up, she stopped walking into his room which was a small blessing, but she would send a servant down to inform him that he was needed upstairs. Which he soon came to realise was at a time when she was getting changed.

He wanted to tell Emily about everything that was going on but after their last encounter he was a little afraid about how Emily would react.

He had saved some money over the years, hopefully that would be enough to get them away from here. He could easily find work elsewhere and provide for Emily, he liked to think he was a strong and capable man, definitely not shy of hard work.

He would speak to the doctor at the earliest opportunity to see if he knew of anywhere or anyone who had some work going.

Fully decided on a course of action, he decided he would speak to Emily tonight.

Getting up he dressed for the day ahead, giving her a soft kiss on the nose. 'Until later, my love,' he said, before leaving his room.

Chapter 7

Opening her eyes Emily stretched out with a big smile on her face. She already knew Henry wouldn't be here so wasn't expecting him. The man always got up at the crack of dawn and was always gone by the time she woke up.

For the first time since she got here, she didn't wake up feeling utterly stone cold freezing, the weather must be changing, she thought feeling happy for the first time in a long time.

Sitting up she saw her usual breakfast tray on the little bedside table, it had all her usual morning food, boiled eggs, toast, cheese, fruit and of course, tea. But this morning there was also a beautiful pink carnation beside the tray.

Picking up the flower first, she raised it to her nose and took a sniff and was pleasantly surprised to find that it smelled utterly gorgeous. It made her visualize a meadow full of different coloured flowers and she wanted to dive right in, unlike the ones in her time that had absolutely no fragrance whatsoever, another thing her time had ruined, she thought.

It was their constant obsession with appearances and quantities that had them messing with things that they had no right messing with, and in the process ended up changing what things should look, taste and smell like.

Placing the flower carefully back down on the table, she adjusted the pillow behind her back before taking her tray.

She had never had breakfast in bed before, she thought while tucking into her toast and eggs, that was until she met Henry.

He was such a thoughtful, caring, loyal man, who did his best to attend to her every need. She had never experienced that before; with Craig it had been all about her attending to his needs.

Thinking back to last night had her smiling all over again. She just had one small regret and that was that it wasn't her first time, because it had obviously been Henry's. He didn't say anything, but she could tell with how uncertain his movements were in the beginning.

But it had been the most amazing night of her life, now that was making love, she thought with a smile.

Oh, she had had sex before but that was it, it was just sex, it was meaningless.

She thought what she had with Craig was love but she had been wrong, she had been in love with the idea of being in love, she knew that now. She had heard that saying before but had never understood it until now, but she finally knew the difference. And what was so funny that had her laughing out loud, was that she had to get hit by lightning and time travel in order to realise that.

How much heartache she would have saved herself if she had just realised that sooner!

Last night had been the real thing and she couldn't wait to tell her friend.

Quickly finishing her meal and practically downing her tea, she jumped out of bed, dressed as quickly as she could, which was much easier and quicker now that she was wearing her own underwear, brushed her hair and ran down the street to the doctor's house, knocking excitedly on the door, maybe a little too loudly. Rose answered the door almost instantly with concern etched on her face.

'Emily! What's the matter?'

'Oh no, nothing's wrong, everything's cool. I actually want to share some exciting news with you,' she said, barely able to contain her smile.

'Oh…' putting a hand to her chest, 'When there's a loud persistent knock on the doctor's door, its usually because someone's really hurt or ill or worse dying.'

'Well, relax Rose, nobody's dying, not right now anyway,' she said stepping in as Rose moved to the side to let her in.

'Let's go in the kitchen, I just made some tea,' Rose said, leading the way down the hall.

'Is the doctor in?' Emily asked, looking around because what she had to say she didn't exactly want the doctor to hear.

'No, he got called upon early this morning. A patient of his from across town has gone into labour.'

'Oh, how comes you're not with him?' she asked, as they sat down at an old wooden table in a nice, cosy kitchen.

'I'm too young,' she replied, as she went about pouring two cups of tea as if that was explanation enough.

'I don't understand.'

'I am not married, neither am I a relative to the woman or a midwife. So, I am simply not allowed to be in the room.'

'But wouldn't the doctor need some help? I'm no expert, but I think it takes more than one person to deliver a baby,' she said.

'He will be alright, a midwife is probably there by now. But he's done it before, delivered a baby when the midwife was delayed.'

Shrugging her shoulders, 'Well, at least the woman's husband will be there, he can always help if the midwife isn't there,' she said.

'Oh no, Miss, men are strictly not allowed in the room when the woman is having herself a baby.'

'What?' she practically shouted.

What the hell! In her time if the man wasn't there, he'll get his balls chopped off.

'You seem so surprised, is it not the same in your time?' she asked, putting the tea down on the table.

'Hell no! Men are allowed, in fact they are expected to be in the same room as the woman in labour. It's the man's job to hold his woman's hand and help her get through the labour, they're even allowed to cut the umbilical cord if they want to.'

Rose paused with a biscuit halfway to her mouth.

'Are you serious?' she asked in a whisper, looking around her like she just learned of a deep dark secret and was checking to see if they had just been heard.

'Is anybody else home?' she asked, she couldn't hear any other voices or footsteps and Rose had already said the doctor was out.

'No, it's just me and the doctor since his wife passed away a few years ago. Why?' she asked, putting a plate of biscuits down on the table and sitting down opposite Emily.

'Oh, nothing. I thought I heard something that's all,' she said, not wanting to upset Rose by telling her she was acting a little paranoid.

'What else are men allowed to do in your time?' she asked, sipping on her tea.

'They're allowed to do whatever they want, as usual. Anyway, I have something really big to tell you about Henry.'

'What is it? Is he alright? Because he was here early this morning and he looked alright.'

Now a few months ago and Emily wouldn't have understood anything of what Rose just said, as she tended to speak very fast whenever she was worried or panicked, which happened to be often. But luckily, Emily got used to her ways and understood everything she said, even when the doctor and Henry didn't.

'No, don't worry, it's nothing like that…What? Wait, Henry was here? When?' she asked, probably sounding worried herself.

'This morning, he came to speak to the doctor.'

'What about?' suddenly curious.

'I don't know, it was very early, and I was still upstairs. But I did hear your name and the doctor saying something about a job.'

'A job?'

'Yes, Miss,' nodding her head.

'What job?' wishing Rose wouldn't be so cryptic.

'I'm not sure, Miss, but I did hear something about a move as well.'

'A move? Who's moving?'

'Yes, a move but please don't ask me anything else for I do not know, I did not hear anything more,' she said, beginning to look flustered.

'It's ok Rose, don't worry,' she said with a small laugh, with the saying, "bless her little cotton socks" coming to mind.

'So, what's this big news you wanted to tell me?' Rose asked, obviously desperate to change the subject and stop the questions. Although she did love asking them!

'Well, me and Henry... you know...'

Rose just stared back at her, sipping on her tea, obviously she didn't know what she was trying to get at.

Suddenly Emily felt bad, Rose was so innocent and although not a child, she somehow had a childlike aura about her that Emily now found quite endearing, however annoying she found it in the beginning.

Also, she felt like a bit of a slag!

'Me and Henry, you know... we made love last night.'

And suddenly she had tea all over the front of her dress, a bit on her chin and obviously in her own teacup which she placed down before grabbing a napkin and patting herself dry.

Meanwhile, Rose continued with her coughing fit after spraying her tea all over Emily.

After what seemed like forever, Rose managed to compose herself enough to ask in a very croaky voice, 'You slept together, Miss? As in, you done the deed?' she asked, whispering and looking around as if not to be heard.

'You do remember we're the only ones here, right?' Emily said, pointing between them.

Clearing her throat, she said in a quiet voice, 'Yes, I know.'

And suddenly putting her hands flat against the table, 'How was it, Miss? Did it hurt? Did you bleed? Tell me all about it?'

Then going bright red like a beetroot when Emily started laughing and said,

'This wasn't my first time Rose.'

'How many times did you…'

'Have sex?' barely holding in a laugh, oh bless her, she thought.

'No, no, I don't want to know, I have no business asking you that Miss…' she said, shaking her head.

'Hey Rose, it's ok. Don't sweat it.'

'Sweat it?'

'It means don't worry about it. In my time this is what women do, we talk about that sort of thing. Usually over a bottle of wine but tea would do,' she said with a smile, then remembered the spraying incident from earlier and pushed her teacup away.

'What do you speak about?' she asked, wide eyed and taking another biscuit, settling herself in for some girl talk.

'Mostly the size of their dicks,' she said, shrugging her shoulders while Rose nearly choked on her biscuit.

Rose was obviously too innocent for that kind of talk, so she would spare her the "oh so delicious" details.

She wasn't stupid, she understood that things were different here and she had no wish to take that sweet innocence away with too much information. Especially information that she didn't need to know, not yet anyway.

'The size, Miss?' she asked through choking.

'Yeah, you know... how big or small, that sort of thing,' she said, flicking her wrist.

'Anyway, but that's not the sort of talk I wanted to have.'

'What kind did you want, Miss?' Rose asked looking confused, just like she usually did whenever Emily started talking.

Henry, too, come to think of it, she really should make the effort to be more careful with the things she says, she thought to herself.

'Oh, Rose,' taking a deep breath.

'I think I love him,' she blurted out and Rose's face suddenly lit up.

'But that's good, Miss.'

But when she saw the concern on Emily's face, 'But what's the matter, Miss?'

'I don't know if he feels the same way, we haven't exactly spoken about it. He was gone when I woke up this morning. Although he did leave me a beautiful pink flower on my breakfast tray this morning,' she said with a smile, remembering the pink carnation.

'Forget the flower, Miss, he wouldn't have done the deed with you if he didn't feel the same way.'

Making Emily smile at the way she whispered, "the deed" and looking around.

'Oh Rose… you have much to learn about men.'

'And women,' she added as an afterthought.

This was obviously her own insecurities and self-doubt talking, especially after everything she had been through with Craig, but somehow deep down she knew that Henry wasn't like all the other guys she had known and that he genuinely cared for her. That was clear to see in everything that he did for her. Bringing her breakfast in bed, giving her that extra slice of her favourite cake, which he soon realised was the Victoria sponge, giving her his socks to wear in bed when her feet were cold, the way he laid down his jacket for her to sit on, in the fields… but did he love her? That was the question she was asking herself.

Suddenly Rose's excited voice pulled her out of her thoughts.

'You'll need to start planning the wedding soon, Miss. Can I help? I've never planned a wedding before, never been to one before, never been invited to one.'

It was a good thing that she hadn't been in that moment sipping on her own tea, as she would have ended up spraying it herself.

'Wow! Hold up there, Rose. No one's getting married. We've only just slept together, and we haven't even started dating yet. Let's just go slow and see what happens.'

Instantly regretting her words, this was a perfect example of the kind of thing she should be careful when speaking about, because Rose just looked like she'd just been slapped in the face.

Standing up Rose started to pace up and down the kitchen, wringing her hands on her apron, a habit it seemed when nervous.

'But you have to, Miss, why wouldn't you marry Henry, he's a nice lad, isn't he? And your reputation will be in tatters, Miss.'

'My reputation?' she asked and started to laugh.

'Oh, you crack me up, Rose,' she said, wiping away the laughter tears that were pouring down her face.

'What's so funny, Miss?' Rose asked in a quiet voice.

And when Emily looked back at Rose and saw the hurt clearly on her face, she stopped laughing.

'Oh, you were being serious,' she said.

She didn't mean to upset Rose, but she also didn't understand why Rose was reacting the way she was.

'Well, yes, Miss. This is no laughing matter,' she said seriously.

'I'm sorry, Rose. But you don't normally marry someone you barely know just because you slept together. People normally date for a couple of years, at least, even live together for a while before deciding to take that next step.'

'Well, pardon me, Miss, but you don't do the deed with a man you barely know. There's a name for women like that!' she said, crossing her arms.

'Rose!'

She couldn't believe what she just heard, and coming from Rose. Especially from Rose! Did she just call her a hooker? That's what it sounded like.

'I'm so sorry, Miss. I didn't mean that, sometimes my mouth just gets carried away with me, please forgive me,' she said, wringing her hands on her apron again.

'It's ok, Rose. I understand...'

'No Miss, I don't think you do,' she said interrupting her.

'I think you are still stuck in your time. You need to realise where you are and how things work around here, you can't be here but still expect life to be the same as the life you left behind. You can't be living in both times at once.'

Wow! What really surprised her was the fact that Rose was right!!

She never embraced this time. She was always showing off to Henry and Rose about things they didn't know, and she did, simply because they didn't exist yet in this time.

It was one thing talking about planes and trains and the bloody internet, but it was another thing entirely talking to Rose about how people behave in the future.

That was certainly nothing to brag about anyway.

And she was right about not being able to live in both times at once, she was here now, and she could no longer behave like it was 2022.

Rose was right, things were indeed different here.

She had been here for a few months now with no idea of how to get back home or even if it was possible. Even the doctor had no idea, and he was a man of science.

The point was, she hadn't adapted to life here and she knew it, just look at how she was dressed, she thought looking down at herself. Oh, she wore the clothes of the time, she wasn't crazy enough to go walking around in her jeans and trainers however much she wanted to, but underneath the dress she wore her own bra and thong instead of the corset she had been given.

She really needed to be more careful, she didn't want to get stoned to death or burned at the stake. Did they even do that here? she wondered. She never did do well in history class, in fact that had been a complete failure.

'You're right, Rose, you're completely right,' she said, defeated.

'I haven't adapted very well, but it's not easy. You have no idea how hard it is knowing everything I know from my time and then being here...' She was beginning to feel tears stinging the back of her throat and took a sip of tea in an attempt to push them back down.

'It's just so different.'

'I can't pretend to understand, Miss, but I can try to help, just like you helped me.'

'What do you mean? I didn't do anything.'

'Yes, you did, Miss. You taught me how to write and read and that means the world to me. It means my freedom! Because, Miss, instead of waiting for when the doctor has time to read to me, which isn't often, I can now read myself, Miss,' she said, smiling with her own tears glistening in her eyes.

'Every night before sleep I read now, and I am no longer me...' tapping at her own chest.

'I am someone else, living somewhere else, doing something else... You see, Miss, I am free! Where before I was not. You gave me that freedom, and for that I would be forever grateful.'

Now they both had tears falling down their cheeks.

Standing up, Emily walked over to where Rose was still standing and pulled her into her arms where they both cried and laughed together.

Eventually wiping their tears away, they sat back down and continued drinking their tea in silence, with Emily noticing that this was the longest Rose had gone without speaking, and she found that she could no longer stand it.

She was never one to care about what people thought of her, but she realised that she did indeed care what Rose and Henry thought of her. One thing she came to dread was them thinking bad of her.

'Rose… I'm truly sorry if I offended you,' she said quietly, looking down at the cup in her hands.

'No Miss, you didn't. It's ok.'

'No Rose, it's not. I don't want you thinking I'm one of those women who sleep around with every Tom, Dick and Harry. Because even though in my time things are different, I've never been the type to sleep around or have one-night stands. I'm no virgin but every time I slept with someone, I was always in a relationship with them.'

'You don't need to explain, Miss, your business is your own.'

'But that's where you're wrong, your opinion means the world to me. You're my friend, Rose, and I don't want you thinking bad of me,' she said, beginning to feel the tears building up again. She was getting very emotional, but this girl meant so much to her.

'I don't think bad of you, Miss, honestly, I don't. I was just a little shocked that's all.'

'Just a little?' raising her eyebrows, trying to make light of the conversation before she started to cry again.

'But I do still think you need to make a decision, and quickly, Miss, because if this gets out...'

'It won't, no one knows apart from me and you and of course, Henry.'

'Oh, the walls have eyes and ears, Miss, especially in that household.'

'What do mean by that? Have you heard anything?' It was certainly an odd thing to say, she thought.

'No, Miss, not about you. But they do love to gossip there, especially the cook's assistant,' she said.

'Okay... anyway, everybody thinks I'm his sister, remember? How do we even explain that one? There are laws about that sort of thing you know, even in this time.'

'Yes, that is quite a pickle,' Rose agreed.

'So, what do you think we should do?'

'Are you asking me for advice, Miss?'

'Well yeah, there isn't anybody else here I can see,' she said while looking around.

'Nobody has ever asked me for advice before or even given much care for my opinion,' she admitted.

'Well, this your time is it not? So, who better to give me some good advice?' she said, pointing out her little finger while sipping on her tea pretending to be posh.

Suddenly Rose went red, and her eyes grew wide.

'Are you ok? You're not choking, are you?' looking down at the half-eaten biscuit in her hand and was about to run over to her when she spoke.

'Erm... Miss... you're drinking the tea,' Rose said, pointing at the cup in her hands.

Emily just stared at her not sure what she was trying to say, Rose was a little odd at times, but this was a little too odd even for her.

'Didn't some of my spit go in there...'

'Oh gross!' putting down the cup and pushing it away, remembering the spraying incident from earlier.

'You scared me, I thought you were choking.'

'No, Miss. I wasn't.'

'Well, I know that now and for crying out loud, stop calling me Miss, you, silly goose.'

'Ok.' And just before sipping her tea she whispered, 'Mrs.'

'I heard that, Rose.'

And they both burst into laughter.

Chapter 8

After leaving the doctor's house, she decided to take a little stroll to the fields to see if Henry was there.

Spending the day with Rose had left her with a lot to think about, as well as leaving her with the impatience to see Henry again.

Spending the day with Rose had also ended up being a lot of fun and teaching her how to make Spaghetti Bolognese had surprisingly turned into a lesson for her too, as they first had to mince the beef in a meat grinder before making their own pasta too.

How easy and convenient they had things in her own time and yet they still found things to complain about, she thought to herself.

But Rose had been right about one thing, well, a couple, if she was going to be brutally honest with herself and especially about her and Henry.

People in this time didn't date like they did back in her time and women didn't sleep with a man out of wedlock, she knew that much from the books that she read. And just like Rose had kindly informed her, there was a name for the kind of women who did.

Wrinkling her nose at that memory, she knew that Rose didn't mean it in that way and that she didn't think of her as a hooker, but it still strangely hurt.

Pushing the memory away, she started to think about Henry and what the next step could possibly be for them. Was Rose right? Did it mean marriage? And was she even ready for that step?

With Craig she thought she was, she believed that she wanted the whole thing, marriage, house, kids. Then the shit hit the fan and she ended up here, met Henry and finally realised that she hadn't actually been in love with Craig!

What if this was the same? What if she wasn't in love with Henry either? How did you know when it was the real deal? What if she just couldn't trust him? That's what she was afraid of, she knew she had some major trust issues and who could really blame her, especially after everything she had been through. And Henry was a good man, he deserved a loving, trusting relationship.

But what if Craig damaged her so much that she could never trust another man again!

The thought made her sad, that she might never have what she craved, what she deserved, what everyone deserved.

She knew she had developed feelings for Henry a while back but wasn't quite sure of his feelings towards her, until last night that was.

She was afraid and she knew it, but she had to stop doubting herself and start to trust again, knew that she couldn't let the past control her anymore.

Henry wasn't Craig, most men weren't like Craig for that matter, he was something altogether unique, she thought, shaking her head.

Reaching the fields, she looked around, there were a few people around, men digging and women either watering their crops or filling their baskets, but there was no sign of Henry.

Before turning to leave she decided to check in on her little willow tree and was happy to see that it was certainly still alive and decided to take that as a good sign.

Sitting down by the little tree, she decided to wait for a bit and see if Henry would turn up. He was usually here by now, but then again maybe she missed him, realising she had spent far longer with Rose than intended. The doctor hadn't been back, and she didn't want to leave Rose alone, she knew all too much about feeling lonely and besides, time flies when you're having fun, and they did have fun. Remembering how Rose laughed so hard she ended up farting, when Emily was trying to stuff the beef in the grinder, not realising she had to cut it into chunks first.

Looking ahead she tried to visualize the place like she knew it to be but found that she couldn't concentrate enough, not with the conversation she had with Rose about marriage going round her head.

Eventually she gave up trying and just watched the people going about their business.

Would Henry expect marriage? she thought.

If what Rose had said was right, then that would be what Henry would want, wouldn't it?

She loved Henry, fair enough it wasn't love at first sight, she thought he was a complete weirdo when she first set eyes on him, but it grew, just like this twig, she thought looking down at it and smiling. This little tree was like her and Henry, she thought. From a little twig they planted, it will grow into a majestic tree, just like their love did.

She could easily imagine herself being Henry's wife, picture them together with a child or two, running around, a real family.

But would she rush into marriage if they were in her time? The answer to that was no, she wouldn't. Not because she doubted her love for this man, she honestly couldn't imagine her life without him. They had spent so much time together the past few months, they were practically inseparable, she would be lost without him. He was literally the air that she breathed, she thought sighing deeply.

But it was too soon after that train crush Craig and you don't marry someone after knowing them only for a few months, despite that being the norm here.

She would just have to speak to Henry about her fears and concerns if he ever mentioned marriage.

Noticing the sun now beginning to set and people were also leaving, she got up and walked back home, looking forward to seeing Henry.

✳✳✳

Walking through the first door, she instantly heard voices coming from Henry's room and one voice in particular she didn't like, hearing it literally gave her goose bumps.

Standing outside and trying to eavesdrop on what they were saying, she heard something about earrings and Henry saying that it wasn't possible. But she was only catching bits of the conversation and couldn't be sure, so she decided to just go in. Nothing was ever gained from eavesdropping anyway, apart from misunderstandings.

Opening the door and walking inside, she saw it was the woman who owned the house. She would never call her the lady of the house, as she often heard Henry and others call her because there was nothing ladylike about her!

'Henry, is everything ok?' she asked, after seeing the sour look on the other woman's face.

'Yes Emily, everything's fine,' he said, after clearing his throat.

Making her wonder what was going on as he clearly looked uncomfortable.

'As I said My Lady, they're not here and if I happen to see them anywhere, I will inform you.'

'Make sure that you do,' she said curtly.

On her way out, she stopped by Emily who was stood by the door and looked her up and down, wrinkling her nose before sticking her chin out and walking out with an evil smirk on her face.

Raising her arm, she took a quick sniff of her armpit. 'Nope, not me,' she said.

'Sorry?'

'I was talking about that bad smell in here, but it's gone now,' she said, a little too loudly, before closing the door behind her. 'I was right when I said that woman's a bitch,' she added, while walking over to Henry.

'Emily... you know it's not lady like to say things like that,' he said with a smirk.

'Henry... you know I'm no lady,' she said, standing on tip toe and giving him a quick peck on the lips.

'Everything ok?' she asked again, now they were alone.

'Yes, everything's fine,' he replied, placing his hand behind his neck and taking a deep breath.

Ok, he was definitely lying to her, she thought to herself. Putting his hand behind his neck was always a move he made whenever he was stressed, and always whenever he was around that woman.

'Are you sure? That looked kind of intense.'

'I'm sure, it was just a misunderstanding. Nothing for you to worry about.'

'What kind of misunderstanding? Because I heard her saying something about earrings.'

'You really are like a dog,' he said, sitting down on the bed and laughing softly.

'Excuse me?' she asked, crossing her arms across her chest and frowning. Did he really just call her a dog?

Realising his mistake, he jumped up off the bed.

'No, no, I didn't mean it in that way,' coming to stand directly in front of her.

'No? And in what way did you mean it?' she asked with her eyebrows raised.

Let's see how he gets out of this one, she thought. Calling her a dog. The fucking cheek!

He looked like he wanted to take her hands at one point, because he reached out but ended up pulling them back again when she refused to uncross them. And coughed to clear his throat instead, another nervous habit of his.

'What I meant was that you don't give up easily when you want something, kind of like a dog with a bone, you never let go. And you have perfect hearing, just like a...'

'Like a dog,' she finished for him.

'Erm, yes like a dog,' he repeated, smiling sheepishly and scratching the back of his head.

They stood there for a few moments just watching each other, of course she didn't really think he meant it in a bad way, but it was just too funny watching him sweat. The poor guy looked petrified, so she decided to give him a break.

Uncrossing her arms, she poked him softly in the belly. 'Just don't call me a dog again, buster,' she said, and instantly saw his eyes light up.

'Phew,' he said, pretending to wipe sweat from his brow.

'So...'

Suddenly Henry pulled her towards him, placing one hand on the small of her back and with the other fisted in her hair, he kissed her long and hard, making her head swirl.

If he hadn't been holding her so tight, she would have been afraid of losing her balance.

Pulling back and looking into her dazed eyes, 'That's better,' he said, still holding her.

'Erm, yeah, yeah that's better,' she said, more than a little flustered.

Well, that was unexpected, she thought. First, he was calling her a dog and the next he was kissing her like there was no tomorrow.

Not to mention that the kiss was a complete contrast to last night's, not that she was complaining though.

Gaining her composure back, she pulled back out of his arms, straightening her dress even though it didn't need fixing but just for something to do.

'So, erm... what was that about anyway?' she asked, needing to clear her own throat.

'The kiss?' he asked, raising one eyebrow.

Damn, but the man looked sexy when he did that.

'No silly,' she said with a laugh and lightly smacking him on the arm.

'What the bitch was moaning about.'

'Oh that,' he said, taking a deep breath and sitting back down on the edge of the bed.

She was beginning to worry now as she could see that he was clearly in distress, as he was now leaning forward with his head in his hands.

If only he would just talk to her.

Coming to sit down beside him, she put a hand on his shoulder.

'Henry, is everything ok? What did she say? And please don't lie to me, I've had a belly full of lies.'

'I'm just trying to protect you,' he said, sitting up now and looking at her so she could see the sincerity in his eyes.

'Protect me from what?' She asked, wondering why she would need protecting and who would want to do her harm in the first place.

She would admit she hadn't adapted well, remembering her earlier conversation with Rose, but she hadn't been walking around shouting about the future like a crazy person and making enemies. Or did she? Beginning to doubt herself and remembering what Rose had said about the walls having ears around here.

Taking her hand in his, he gave it a kiss before resting both their hands together on his leg.

'She came down here this evening to ask how long you will be staying here, she very kindly reminded me of the fact that I said it would only be for a few weeks and it's now been a few months instead.'

So that was it, she wanted her out.

Well, she couldn't exactly blame her, it was her house after all. And it wasn't like she worked for her like Henry did or even paid rent, so why would she let her stay.

But suddenly her heart sunk at the thought of not seeing Henry every day, she wasn't the clingy type, but he worked such long hours that if they weren't living together, she would hardly ever see him.

She couldn't imagine not seeing his face at night before going to sleep, couldn't imagine not waking up to the feather light kisses he started giving her on the top of her head, which started exactly a month ago when he thought she was sleeping.

Her heart broke at the thought of losing those sweet tender moments.

And where would she even go? It wasn't like she had any money to pay rent with. Perhaps the doctor would let her stay for a while, at least until she figured stuff out, like a job for starters.

Feeling a squeeze on her hand, she looked up to find Henry watching her.

'Hey, you look like you're a million miles away,' he said.

'Yeah, a million miles into the future,' she said with a smile that obviously didn't reach her eyes.

'Hey, talk to me,' he said, tucking gently at her hand.

'I don't know, Henry. If this was my time, I wouldn't have been so worried, I would have known what to do. Everything would have been so different, I would have had a job and my own place to begin with, I wouldn't have been so dependent on you. What am I going to do now? Where would I even go?'

She realised she was beginning to sound panicked and desperate but that was because she was, and she hated that. It suddenly hit her and perhaps it should have been her first thought, that as well as not seeing Henry every day, she actually had nowhere to go, and no job.

She would literally be homeless, and homelessness was never pretty, but in this place and time, it was much worse than anything she had ever seen back home. She would never survive!

'Hey, don't worry. She hasn't done anything yet.'

'But she will,' she said quietly, looking down at his hand holding hers and feeling the urge to hold on tighter but she also didn't want to show any weakness. She didn't want him thinking less of her.

'Listen to me Emily, I don't want you to worry about anything. I will figure something out.'

'How?' she asked, beginning to feel the tears building up and trying her best to keep them down.

'We will leave, together,' he stated firmly.

'But what about your job? Your life? And where would we even go?' shaking her head. 'No, I can't ask you to do that for me, you can't give up your life here for me. It's not fair on you, it's not right,' she said, pulling back her hands. 'I'm not worth it,' she added.

Reaching out, he cupped her cheeks in both hands and wiped away the tears that she didn't realise were falling down her face until now.

'You are worth it!' he said, looking deep into her eyes trying to make her see the truth in his. 'You are everything to me.'

Which only caused to make her cry even more.

'You can't say that, you barely know me,' she said through her tears

'I know enough,' he said, giving her head a gentle shake.

'We will figure this out, ok?'

Nodding her head, he pulled her towards him where he kissed the top of her head and held her close until her tears had stopped.

Once calm and back to her normal self again, she started to think back to the bits of conversation she had heard between Henry and that woman.

She was sure she heard her mention something about earrings but didn't catch the whole conversation, but what she found interesting was that Henry had somehow avoided answering that question. That he probably kissed her in order to distract her!

Pulling back, 'By the way, what was that she was saying about earrings?' she asked, making Henry laugh.

'Yeah, yeah, I know. I'm just like a dog with a bone,' saying it for him.

'Believe it or not, it's what I love the most about you,' he said, giving her a peck on the nose.

Did he just say what she thought he just said? That he loves her? She thought to herself, while doing a mental dance inside her head, screeching, "he loves me, he loves me", like a teenager.

'Did you just say the L word?' she asked. Well, she wanted to be sure she heard right, didn't she? She was sure of her feelings for him, she just wasn't sure of his. As she mentioned to Rose earlier, they didn't exactly have that talk, did they?

'The L word?' he asked, raising that sexy eyebrow again.

'Yeah, you know. Love,' whispering that last word, making Henry laugh.

'I've never laughed so much until I met you,' he said, putting a strand of her hair behind her ear, making her heart skip a beat at the contact.

'So, you're saying I'm a clown now, huh?'

'A very beautiful clown,' he said, leaning towards her.

Her breath hitched in her throat when she realised he was about to kiss her, with her heart fluttering, she jumped up off the bed and out of his way.

Oh, she wanted the kiss alright and much more in fact, but she wouldn't be distracted a second time.

'Hey, no distractions, buster,' she said, wagging a finger at him.

'Come on Henry, what are you keeping from me?' she asked again, after seeing him take a deep breath.

It must be something serious if he's worried about telling her, she thought.

'Come, sit down and I'll tell you everything.'

She hesitated for a while, not sure if it was going to be another distraction.

Until he looked her in the eyes and said, 'Please, Emily.'

Sitting back down next to him, she couldn't help feeling nervous. Why couldn't he tell her when she was standing? Usually, it was almost always bad news when someone asked you to sit down first. What could possibly be so bad that she had to sit down.

'Listen Emily, I would like you to try and stay out of her way as much as possible, until we figure this out.'

'Agreed, and I have been by the way. I'm either stuck in this room or I'm down the road with Rose. I've never once gone near her or upstairs for that matter.'

'I know...'

'And why is she so bothered by me anyway? What's her problem with me? And don't deny it, because I know she has one, every time she sees me, she looks at me like I'm shit on her shoes.'

'Her problem is simply that I am not alone,' he said.

'I don't understand, Henry. What do you mean? She doesn't even know who I am, she thinks I'm your sister.'

'Yes, but you are still here, in my room, in my life.'

'Ok, you're going to have to do better than that, because I haven't got a clue as to what you're trying to say to me.'

Henry clearly looked agitated, which made her wonder what the hell was going on around here and if she was honest, all sorts of thoughts were running around in her head.

She knew the woman was married, she had seen her out in public with a man and with her arm linked through his and when she asked Rose about him, she found out he was her husband. To tell the truth, she had been quite surprised to hear that at the time, as she had assumed the man was her father, he was clearly a good few years older than her.

Obviously, she had married him for his money and this big house. Dirty little gold digger, she thought to herself.

But what was going through her mind this very second was if Henry and that woman had ever been lovers before she got married, or worse, were they having an affair until she turned up?

Was that why she wanted her gone so badly? So, they could pick up where they left off?

The very thought of Henry with that woman had her stomach twisted into knots.

If that was the case, then what about Henry and herself? What did that mean for them? They slept together last night, and he just said he loved her. And thinking of last night, she could have sworn it was his first time.

'I think she's trying to accuse you of stealing her earrings. She says they've suddenly gone missing.'

To say she was shocked was a huge understatement.

'I thought you were going to say...'

'Say what?'

Shaking her head in shock, 'It was nothing, forget it. But why, why would she say something like that?'

'You do know I would never do anything like that, don't you?' she asked, suddenly afraid Henry would think her a thief.

'Emily, it had never even entered my mind that you would do something like that!' he said, giving her hand a reassuring squeeze, and bringing it up to his lips where he planted a tender kiss in her palm and held it to his cheek for a while, before bringing it back down.

Shaking his head now, 'I really don't know how or where, to even begin.'

'I'm starting to get really worried now, Henry, so start talking, will you?'

Nodding his head, he took a deep breath.

'It started a short while before you came. I have been working for her husband for a number of years and when they married, we all knew it wasn't for love but for the money, the house, the status, all the things this sort of people care about.'

'I knew it!' she blurted out.

'And?' she prompted.

'And everything was fine until a few months ago, when she suddenly started to come into my room, uninvited and without warning...'

'What do you mean? She would sneak in when you weren't here?'

Remembering that day when she had just finished getting dressed and the door opened and in she walked.

'Not exactly.'

'Then what?' she asked, she couldn't imagine her trying to steal anything from Henry, because he clearly didn't have anything worth stealing.

'She would come in when she knew I would be here. Always at the same time, when she knew I would be back from the fields and getting changed.'

'What!' she couldn't believe what she just heard, for once in her life she was speechless.

'Obviously, when you turned up that stopped, but it didn't stop completely.'

Getting up he walked over to the desk and poured out two glasses of water from a jug, walking back to the bed, he handed one to Emily and sat back down next to her.

'Recently she had been sending for me, upstairs, pretending something needs fixing or she needs my help moving something.'

'Let me guess, whenever her husband isn't around?'

'You guessed right,' he said, drinking his water.

'That's sexual harassment, you do know that, right?' she told him.

'Her husband is never around, he's always locked away upstairs in his office and when he's not working, his at his gentlemen's club and doesn't get back until late in the night.'

'Well, if her own husband avoids her, then that tells you something doesn't it?' she said, trying to put herself in her shoes and thinking how lonely she must feel. Hell, she had been in her shoes, how many nights did she spend home alone waiting for that bastard to come home. But that was no excuse!

'But that's no excuse for what she's been doing Henry. You don't start sexually harassing your staff just because you're lonely.'

She could really do with a drink right about now, she thought to herself as she downed her glass of water, while trying really hard to imagine it was a shot of tequila instead.

'And now she's trying to find a reason to kick you out, that's why she's trying to accuse you of stealing from her.'

'But that doesn't make sense. It's her house, she can ask me to leave anytime she wants, she doesn't need a reason.'

'That the thing Emily, she can't. Yes, she's the lady of the house, but it's her husband's house, not hers. And I have worked for her husband long before she married him...'

'So, she has no say over who stays and who goes?' she said, interrupting him.

'That's correct.'

'Wow... Well, that must suck, for her!' making Henry smile.

'So, if he was to find out what a slag his wife is and divorce her, she would finally get the house wouldn't she?' Thinking that maybe she was behaving this way because she wanted to get caught, wanted a divorce so she could have the house, the money. That was after all why she married him, wasn't it?

'That's a strange question to ask, why would you assume she would get the house?' he asked, frowning.

'Well, wouldn't she?' she asked, frowning back.

'No, she wouldn't.'

'Oh ok... Because in my time, when a couple divorce, the woman almost always gets the house and half the money, especially if they have kids.'

'Really?' he asked, clearly surprised at what he just heard.

'Yeah. I'll take it from the look on your face, it's not like that here.'

Wishing she had concentrated more in history class, it would have come in handy.

'No. For one, I don't know anyone who has gotten a divorce, it's just not done, no matter how unhappy a marriage is. And certainly, the woman doesn't get the house and half the money,' he said, laughing and shaking his head at the thought.

'So, what happens to the kids?'

'I truly don't know, I suppose they remain with the father in the house. As I said, I don't know anyone who has gotten a divorce and it's not a subject freely spoken about,' he explained.

'Wow. That's all you hear about in my time.'

'You mean it is a common practice in your time?'

'Hell, yeah. You always read that some celebrity got drunk and got married, only to get divorced a few months later. I, myself, know two people who got divorced.'

'That's sad. A marriage should be for life.'

'Sad but true, unfortunately.'

'How times change,' he said, staring into space.

'Anyway, so you think she's trying to accuse me of stealing, so she can have a reason to get me kicked out?'

'Yes, I think so.'

'Well, can't say I blame her really. I wouldn't want to share you,' she said, giving him a smile when he looked at her.

'So, what do we do now?' she asked, hoping Henry would think of something before she got her arse kicked out. It all made sense now, why she disliked her so much from the very first time she laid eyes on her.

It's because she wanted Henry all to herself.

'We'll leave this place,' he said with determination.

'And go where?'

'I'm not sure yet, but wherever we go, we should go soon. I don't trust her.'

Maybe she should just go, she thought. It seems like she had been nothing but a headache for Henry ever since she got here, with her relentless questions, her refusal to accept things and behave like everyone else, and now this.

And after hearing that Henry had worked here for years and he was secure, she didn't think it was fair to expect him to up and leave with her.

Maybe she could have a quite word with that bitch before leaving, and threaten to tell her husband everything, maybe that would fix Henry's problem. She didn't want to just leave without trying to help.

'Henry, maybe it would be best if I was to just leave...'

'What? No!'

'I just don't think it's fair for you to get up and leave everything and everyone you know because of me. You have known these people a lot longer than you've known me.'

Grabbing her face with both hands and forcing her to look him in the eyes,

'This place means nothing to me without you. Nothing, absolutely nothing will keep me apart from you,' he said.

And for the first time in her life, she saw it, love.

It was a look she had always longed to see, a feeling she had always longed to feel but had only ever read about. And she had to travel how many God damn years into the past to find it!

The thought made her smile, fate really did work in mysterious ways.

'Ok,' she said, nodding her head and smiling with fresh tears in her eyes. But these were not sad tears, for the first time in her life she experienced the tears of joy, that she had only ever seen so much of in the movies, and never believed were possible.

And she saw him release a sigh of relief, before he took her in his arms and kissed her.

Chapter 9

Waking up the next morning, she stretched out her arms and legs with a big smile on her face, then curled back up under the blanket feeling truly happy for the first time in her life.

While she was lying there feeling utterly content, the conversation she had with Rose the previous day about marriage popped into her head.

Yesterday, she had been a bit reluctant about the possibility of getting married so soon, but after last night... well, let's just say that if Henry was to get down on one knee and propose, she wouldn't say no.

Laughing out loud and pulling the blanket up over her face, shy at her own thoughts.

She had actually found it, love!

And this time the man she loved with all her heart, loved her back!

She could easily picture them together in a little cottage, Henry working their own land, with her cooking and baking in the kitchen, with apple pies coming to mind.

She had always loved baking and she couldn't wait to have her own kitchen.

And obviously that picture wouldn't be complete without a couple of kids running around, three would be the perfect number, a boy and two girls. She could picture the boy being the oldest and the little girls with pink ribbons tied around their little pigtails, running around the garden and jumping all over Henry.

It was the perfect picture, the perfect life.

She must have fallen asleep at some point with that picture in her mind, because she dreamt of the most cutest, gorgeous boy she had ever seen. With blond hair that was a little too long and bright blue eyes, laughing while running around a tree, a willow tree, being chased by someone she couldn't see.

Woken up by a sound just outside the door, she sat up just in time to see the door opening and the bitch from hell stepping right in.

Obviously by her reaction she hadn't been expecting to see her still here and in bed, because she looked visibly startled at seeing her.

'Oh, I didn't know you were in,' she said, sounding flustered.

' 'Course you didn't,' Emily replied while rubbing the sleep from her eyes. It was so strange that the more sleep you got, the more tired you felt, when it should have been the other way around.

'Can I help you with something?' Emily asked, after seeing her awkwardly looking around the room. What the hell was she doing here anyway, she knew Henry wouldn't be here.

'What are you doing in bed at this time? It's nearly time for lunch,' she stated, looking down at her after gaining her composure from being caught sneaking into the room.

'I don't think that's any of your concern, do you?' Emily replied with a smile, just to irritate her. What's it got to do with her anyway, who died and made her queen of England, she thought sourly.

God, she couldn't stand the woman from the beginning but after what Henry told her last night, she bloody hated her.

'Well, when you're under my roof...'

'Don't worry love, I won't be under your roof for much longer.'

'I'm pleased to hear Henry has finally come to his senses, you have distracted him quite enough the past few months.'

'Oh, don't worry about Henry. He'll be coming with me.'

'Excuse me?' she said, frowning down at her.

Obviously, she hadn't been expecting to hear that.

'Your excused,' Emily said, feeling quite proud of herself.

Huh, got you there, you, dumb bitch, she thought when seeing her standing there with her mouth gaping open.

'Well, I never...'

'Yeah, neither have I, but what can you do?' she said, raising her eyebrows and shrugging her shoulders.

'Now, if you'll excuse me, I have to get dressed,' she said, getting out of bed and standing there in just Henry's shirt which was just long enough to reach the top of her thighs.

'Is that Henry's shirt?' she asked, pointing a shaking finger towards her.

'Yeah, looks good on me, doesn't it?' she said, doing a little twirl and coming back round to face her.

The two of them just stared at each other for what seemed to Emily like forever, before the other woman turned and walked out slamming the door behind her.

Phew, Emily thought, letting out a breath that she hadn't realised she was holding in.

There was something about the way that woman stared at her, the look in her eyes, it gave her goose bumps.

The quicker they got away from her the better.

While getting dressed she thought about the dream she had, it had been a beautiful, joyous dream, but it also felt strange.

Unlike the usual dreams you have where you are actually in them and the main character, this one felt like she was floating above and looking down at the scene below.

The boy looked like a young Henry and the willow tree was the one she knew so well. Was it a sign that everything would be ok and that she and Henry would live happily ever after?

She had always been a great believer in dream interpretation and that some dreams are meant to guide us, so she decided to take it as a good sign.

Once she finished getting dressed, which took a while because she had to wear the corset instead of her bra. How did these women do it? She wondered, day in and day out.

She didn't think she would ever get used to wearing this thing.

Well, one thing was for sure, she couldn't continue wearing her bra anymore, because the wire had come out of its stitches and started to poke her between her breasts. If she continued wearing it, she was afraid she would get staked in the heart like a vampire.

She quickly downed the tea Henry had left her, which by now had turned stone cold and decided to skip the toast after poking a finger at it, as cold toast was never appealing, and went for an apple on her way out instead.

She decided to go for a walk first then go and see Rose. She had promised to teach her how to make her famous brownie recipe today. That's if the doctor didn't keep her too busy.

She had grown very fond of Rose and the doctor and couldn't imagine going a day without seeing them.

Walking down the local market she thought about how much her life had changed, how much she had changed since coming here. Getting struck by lightning and coming here had ended up being the best thing to ever happen to her.

If she had a choice of going back or staying here, what would she choose if faced with that decision? Would she stay or would she go?

Then the tune, "should I stay or should I go", started playing in her head.

She might not like the clothes, the lack of technology, especially having no internet and phone and let's not forget McDonald's, but she was happy here.

Happier than she'd ever been in her time, in fact.

For the first time in a very long time, she was happy and could imagine a future, she had Henry and her friends, she didn't need anything else.

Walking past a jewellery shop, she stopped when her eyes caught a pocket watch in the glass display. It looked like it was made from yellow gold and had Roman numerals with a little wind-up key attached by a short chain.

That would definitely suit Henry, she thought while walking into the shop.

After asking for the price, she was pleased to realise she had enough money to buy the watch, as she had saved up all the money Henry had given her for helping him out in the fields. She had resisted at first, telling him she could earn her own money and that she was a modern, independent woman. Until he very cleverly pointed out, it was exactly what she had been doing, earning her own money by working in the fields with him. So, she eventually accepted the money while knowing it was coming out of his own wages.

So, she had saved it all, not spending even a penny on herself and today she was glad for that.

Stepping out of the jewellery shop, she stood for a moment and admired the pocket watch she now held in her hands.

It was so beautiful and so Henry, she could easily picture him pulling it out of his trouser pocket and checking the time.

The man was obsessed with time, she didn't think he was ever late for anything in his life. Just like herself, she thought with a smile.

Taking a closer look at the watch, she noticed something that she didn't notice in the shop, as the man wouldn't let her hold it until she had paid for it first. Not that she could blame him for being wary, it wasn't like they had security cameras or even security guards and the poor man didn't look fit or healthy enough to chase anyone down the street.

Bringing it up closer she saw that it had a little six petal flower engraved on the wind-up key, it was so tiny but so pretty, she couldn't wait to give it to Henry.

Popping it back in her purse with a smile, she set off to the doctor's house.

✳✳✳

After a very quick visit to see Rose and show her the pocket watch she got for Henry, which quickly gained the approval from both the doctor and Rose, she headed back up the street to find Henry. It turned out the doctor was having a very busy day and couldn't do without Rose today, so they decided to leave the brownie baking for tomorrow, something the doctor made her promise to.

Walking back up the street, she wished she had some paper to wrap the watch up with. She had always loved Christmas but not for the reason most people would think. What she loved the most about that holiday was actually giving the gifts, wrapping them up in pretty glittery paper and seeing the people she loved opening them up on Christmas morning.

She was the type of person that started doing the Christmas shopping in the summer as she didn't want to be left disappointed when the things she wanted were sold out by December, which they usually were by that point, and not to mention the prices always went up then too.

Oh, she couldn't wait for her and Henry's first Christmas together!

She was aware it was going to be very different this time and not at all what she was used to, but she couldn't wait.

Walking with that thought in mind and smiling like a silly clown, she didn't notice the brown leather suitcase that was outside Henry's door and tripped over it, landing flat on her face.

It felt like an explosion of pain across her entire face and head. Pushing herself up with her hands she saw the blood drip down on the floor.

Sitting up, she put a hand to her nose and realised she must have broken it as the blood seemed to be pouring out, and for a few seconds was almost blinded from the tears in her eyes.

'Fuck!' she said out loud.

Picking up the purse she dropped when she fell, she slowly stood up.

She would have to head back to the doctor's house if it was broken, and from the amount of blood that she could see, she could safely say that it was.

At least she didn't have to go far, because he was only down the street, she thought.

Taking the shawl from her shoulders, she used one end to put to her nose, because the last thing she wanted was her blood all over her dress, it wasn't like she had many clothes now, was it? And the last thing anyone in this house wanted, was her blood all over the floor.

Gathering her composure and blinking away the tears that just didn't seem to want to stop, she placed the fallen suitcase upright against the wall, after knocking it down and smashing her face on the floor and wondered what the hell it was doing there in the first place.

What kind of idiot just left a suitcase in the middle of the hallway?

Taking a deep breath and doubling the layer of the shawl against her nose, she opened the door, stepped in and froze.

Instantly the memory of Craig and that whore came flashing back in her mind, because right there before her a very similar scene was playing out in front of her very eyes.

Chapter 10

Stood frozen where she stood, she couldn't believe what she was just seeing.

That woman lying on Henry's bed, with Henry on top of her, locked in a kiss!

Her heart felt like it had stopped beating and dislodged itself from its position in her chest and fell straight down into her stomach.

Putting a hand to her stomach, she took a deep breath that didn't feel like it had reached her lungs.

Never in a million years would she have thought that Henry was capable of such betrayal, especially after everything he had said last night.

But men it seemed were all the same, they just couldn't keep it in their pants!

She must have made some sort of noise or said something without realising, because Henry suddenly pulled back and standing up, he looked in her direction with shock clear on his face.

He obviously hadn't been expecting her despite her staying here with him.

Well, not anymore. She would rather sleep in the filthy streets than be anywhere near these two!

'Emily...'

'No, no, no, no, no.......' shaking her head.

'This isn't happening, not again,' she whispered to herself.

Henry took a few steps towards her reaching out, but she slapped his hands away.

'Don't touch me, don't you dare come anywhere near me,' she shouted at him.

She was shaking so much that she was surprised that she managed to get the words out at all, never mind shout them.

'Emily, please. It's not what you think,' he said, pleading with her to listen.

'It's exactly what I think, I'm not blind,' she said, practically screaming the words at him.

'Em...'

Reaching out towards her again, she pulled back so quickly, she ended up banging her elbow on the wall behind her.

'I said don't touch me!' looking him up and down in disgust.

'You're just like all the others.'

'Now, why would your sister be so mad at us Henry? I wonder,' she said, tapping her chin in mock curiosity.

Looking past Henry and seeing her still lounging on the bed, propped up on one elbow with her hand supporting her head, watching them.

She was definitely enjoying the show, that was sure.

She wanted to smack that smirk right off her face!

'Oh, shut up, you, slag. You know full well I'm not his sister,' she screamed at her.

At Emily's outburst she started to laugh, it was a loud screechy laugh, the type that made your skin crawl and think of fingernails on a chalk board.

That was when Henry surprised her by turning round to the other woman and in a voice cold of any emotion, said, 'I think you should leave. I think you've caused enough trouble, don't you?'

Tilting her head to one side and standing, 'Are you kicking me out of my own house, Henry?' she asked, staring him right in the eyes.

'No, my lady. Just out of my room,' he replied with determination, with his head held high.

'We said what we had to say to each other, now I need to speak to Emily,' he added.

The only reason she was still standing here rooted to the spot, and watching this little exchange between them, was because her legs had turned to jelly the second she had laid eyes on them.

It wasn't like the time she had caught Craig with another woman, that was different. She had known deep down that he had been cheating on her and had expected to catch him out eventually. But obviously not in the way that she did and certainly not in their bed!

It had still been a shock but not enough to render her immobile, like she found herself now.

She had to get her shit together and move, not just stand here in front of them.

'Emily...'

'You lied to me. Everything you said, it was all a lie,' she said, staring at him and shaking her head in disbelief.

'It wasn't a lie, let me explain,' he said.

'I'm so stupid, how could I have fallen for the same shit twice?' she said to herself.

'Emily...'

Again, Henry tried to reach out towards her but in the moment, she found her strength and pushed him back with her free hand.

'I told you, don't touch me,' she yelled, hearing laughter coming from behind Henry.

'And we have nothing to talk about. We have nothing,' she added.

She turned to leave but Henry grabbed her arm and spun her round.

'Do not walk away from...' and stopped dead in his tracks when he saw her bloody face for the first time, after pulling at the arm that was holding the shawl which was shielding part of her face.

'Emily... what happened?' giving her arm a painful squeeze when she didn't answer.

'Tell me. Did someone do this to you?' he asked more forcefully.

Pulling her arm out of his grasp, 'Don't pretend you care, I've seen your true colours so you can drop the act.'

And looking over his shoulder.

'You're welcome to him, love,' she said to the woman who had just destroyed her dreams.

And with that she turned and ran out of the room.

Hearing Henry shout out her name, she continued to run until she was outside the large front gates, where she saw a wooden crate full of what looked like bottles of wine.

The bitch must be having one of her parties again, she thought. Well, at least now Henry can attend and not pretend to be upset about the noise coming from upstairs, like he so often did. They can drink and dance and shag to their heart's content, she thought, picturing them together and feeling the bile rise from her stomach and into her throat.

And with that thought in mind, she picked up a bottle and continued to run.

Without a thought or plan in place, she found herself in the fields and realised that in her pain, she had run to the little twig that was to grow into her favourite willow tree.

Throwing herself beside it, she pulled her knees up and wrapped her arms around them and cried until she could cry no more.

It hurt and she wasn't just thinking about her face, although her forehead hurt like hell, and it felt like her eyeballs were going to pop out of her head.

No, the type of pain she was really feeling was not the physical type but rather the emotional one instead.

Opening the bottle of wine, she saw it was a white. She never really drank wine as she had always found it too sweet and it always made her feel sick, not to mention that it always seemed to get her wasted far quicker than anything else. It just didn't seem to agree with her.

But what the hell, this was a special occasion after all, wasn't it?

Not everyone walks in on their man over another woman, twice!

Saluting the little twig by her side, she took a big swig.

She was surprised to find how strong it was, almost like paint thinner, not that she ever tasted that, it wasn't like she had a death wish or anything but exactly what she could imagine it tasting like. Just the smell was enough to get you drunk, she thought, taking another swig and coughing.

She must look like a right state right now, sitting here by herself, by a little twig and drinking from a bottle. And let's not forget how her face was covered in blood, she probably looked like something out of a horror movie, she thought, laughing out loud.

Thank God, nobody was here to see her, which felt strange as the place was usually busy with people tending or checking their crops, but there was not one person around.

Probably because it looked like it was going to rain cats and dogs soon, she thought to herself as she looked up at the sky and seeing the fast-approaching clouds.

Halfway through the bottle, she started to think about how the hell she ended up here again, being cheated on, twice or more accurately, finding out twice!

But did Henry really cheat on her?

They weren't exactly dating now, were they? Not technically.

It wasn't like he took her out for dinner or drinks or to the movies now, was it? 'Because the movies don't even exist yet, you, stupid cow!' she said to herself, taking another swig and laughing out loud.

What a fucking joke, her life had turned out to be!

They had slept together once and it was Rose who had put the idea of marriage in her head, not Henry.

Henry never mentioned anything about marriage, nothing, 'Zilch,' she said, pointing her finger at no one.

She realised she was already a little tipsy but carried on drinking anyway. For one, it didn't taste so bad after a while and second, the more she drank the more things made sense, and the less it hurt.

Whoever had said drinking only made things worse had been talking out of their arse, she thought with a giggle and taking another long swig. And an image of a donkey wriggling his bum suddenly came to mind, making her laugh and she couldn't stop laughing until the laughter tears eventually turned in to real gut-wrenching tears.

She thought she could be happy here, in this place, in this time, but the truth was it wasn't the place or the time. It was Henry she loved and without him she didn't want to be here anymore.

At first, she secretly thought it might be a rebound thing, but she very quickly realised that it was the real thing, the real deal, true love at last.

Well, for her at least. Obviously, it was all a lie on his end, or was it? She wondered, thinking back to last night. He didn't actually say he loved you now, did he? She thought to herself.

He called her a dog! Remembering bits of the conversation they had.

He said he loved that the most about her, he didn't say he loved her!

Just that he loves dogs!

Reaching inside her purse, she got out the pocket watch she got for Henry and remembered the dream she had this morning. The dream of the little blond boy running around the tree, her daydreams of her and Henry together as a family in their own home. Looking down at the pocket watch she held in one hand, she started to cry fresh tears at the feeling of loss, at the loss of what could have been.

Why did life have to be so damn hard!

Was this how it was always going to be? If so, she didn't want it. She was tired of the pain.

If only this wasn't the real world and she would wake up one day and realise this was all a bad dream, and she actually had a happy life.

Maybe life was one long, bloody nightmare and we would all wake up from it one day, she thought, downing the rest of the bottle and throwing it as far as she could.

Lying down on the grass and looking up at the dark clouds which were now gathering thick and fast, she felt like she was on a rollercoaster ride and closed her eyes against that feeling. But found that was also a bad idea, as she now felt like she was falling down a deep black hole, headfirst, prompting her to open her eyes wide and take a deep breath.

This was the worst part of getting drunk, the part that made you feel like you were dying, she thought.

As she turned her head to the side, looking at the pocket watch still in her hand, she barely registered the first rain drop as she let go of the watch and closed her eyes.

***

'Emily?'

She could feel herself being shaken and hear someone saying her name.

'Emily, wake up. Can you hear me?'

The shaking intensified, making her feel sick.

'Please wake up.'

Why? She didn't want to wake up. She was so tired, why couldn't she just be left alone.

She could feel herself floating and someone saying, 'I've got you, my love.'

She knew that voice, she loved that voice, that voice made her sad, she thought as she went back to sleep.

Chapter 11

Sitting in the chair beside the bed, stroking her hair back from her forehead with one hand and holding on to her hand with the other, he was glad she had finally settled into a deep sleep.

Seeing her like that, eyes closed and not moving in the freezing cold rain, with that empty bottle not far from her feet, he honestly thought she was dead.

That thought alone had him throwing himself to his knees and shaking her like a madman possessed, until she let out a little moan in protest and he realised, while thanking God and the universe that she was still alive.

Picking her up in his arms, he quickly carried her here to the doctor's, where they now were.

Sitting her up, the doctor had prepared a solution for her to drink, while explaining to Henry that it was better out than in, as what she had drunk was indeed very strong and she had obviously had the whole bottle.

Of course, she had protested at first, but after a couple of sips had ended up vomiting all that she had drunk, and finally settled into the deep sleep she was currently in.

The doctor had also managed to fix her nose and had assured him there would be no lasting damage. Just some swelling for a while to go with the two black eyes she also had, which the doctor explained was because of the hit she took to the bridge of her nose.

Sitting back in his chair, he shook his head and wondered how in the world they had ended up here, and not for the first time since finding her in this state.

Obviously, she had thought he had given in to some sexual urge with that vile woman like a lot of men would have, but what she didn't understand about him was that he wasn't like most men.

He didn't get turned on simply because a woman fluttered her eyelashes at him, in fact it was quite the opposite. And nothing was worse than a woman trying too much and especially a married woman trying to stray from her marriage, no matter how unhappy that marriage may be.

He couldn't just sleep with a woman he didn't have feelings for, which was how he knew he had developed feelings for Emily, when he started having hard-on's simply by just hearing her voice.

How could she think that he would do such a thing, did she not know him at all!

Raking a hand through his hair in frustration before putting his head in his hands in despair.

He had failed her, that was the bottom line, the reason why she was here in this state.

He should have put a stop to that woman's behaviour long before Emily even showed up. He was a coward, plain and simple.

He had a roof over his head, a job, food in his belly and he was worried about losing all of that. Jobs weren't exactly easy to come by.

He knew that woman was trouble from the very beginning, as almost immediately after marrying into the household she started to boss them all around. It was the poor kitchen staff he felt sorry for, the salt was either not enough or too much, the sandwiches were not cut right, the scones were too dry, that was until she set her eyes on him!

'Damn it!' he said out loud, jumping out of his seat so suddenly he caused the chair to topple backwards.

Setting it back up, he walked around the room feeling like a complete failure, a coward and thinking that maybe he didn't deserve Emily.

She deserved somebody who was just as strong as her, just as brave, somebody who was her equal and sadly he was not.

The moment he realised he was in love with her, he should have packed their bags and left that house.

This was all his doing!

Sitting back down, he took hold of her hand in both of his and placed a long tender kiss on her palm before resting his head against her hand.

He had planned on marrying her, to propose with the hope that she would say yes, he had even bought a ring, for Christ's sake!

He had given it to the doctor for safe keeping, as it had crossed his mind that it wasn't very wise to keep it in his room, not with that vile woman walking in whenever it suited her.

He had even found a job, with the doctor's help of course, who had a friend in need of a handyman. They even had a small cottage on the grounds which came with the job.

It had been perfect for them and now it was all perfectly ruined, for he didn't think that Emily would want to marry him now or have anything to do with him for that matter, unless he somehow managed to convince her that he was innocent.

And how the hell was he going to do that?

He must have dozed off at some point because he found himself being woken by a sound. Lifting his head off Emily's hand he looked up and saw it was Rose coming into the room.

Coming in, she pulled up another chair and seated herself down on the other side of the bed.

He quietly watched her touch Emily's forehead with the back of her hand, which he presumed was just out of habit with her being a nurse, because it wasn't like Emily was sick now, was she? No, she instead nearly drank herself to death.

Watching her then take her hand and seeing a single tear fall down her cheek before she quickly wiped it away.

'You two became very close, didn't you?' he asked.

He knew they spent quite some time together and that Rose had shown her how to crochet, as Emily had spent many evenings on her new hobby and was very pleased with herself to finally present him with a scarf. One end was narrower than the other, but he wore it with pride because it was made by her.

But he didn't realise how close they had become.

'Yes, we did,' she said, looking down at her friend with a sad smile.

'I never had a real friend before, if anything happens to her...' stopping herself because she was desperately trying to hold back the tears.

'She will be alright, she's strong,' he said to Rose, feeling the need to comfort her while needing it himself.

'She has to be,' he added, looking back down at Emily and giving her hand another squeeze before bringing it to his lips to plant another kiss.

Looking at her now, she looked so fragile, she was so white and cold, what if she wasn't strong enough? He wondered, but no, he couldn't think that way, she was strong, she would be ok. She had to be because the alternative didn't bear thinking about.

They both fell into a silence, both lost in their own thoughts, then Rose spoke.

'What happened Henry?' she asked.

Looking up he saw she was watching him, he heard her speak but didn't register what she said.

'Pardon?'

'Sorry to intrude on your personal life, maybe it's not my place to say but she is my friend, so maybe it is, my place that is. But I don't think she would have been in this state if she was happy and the last time I had seen her she was happy and couldn't wait to show you what she had gotten you.'

That must be the pocket watch he found in her hand, he thought.

But before he could say anything, she spoke again. 'Again, I do apologise for speaking out of place, but she helped me, she taught me how to write and read...' looking back down at her friend, she continued with tears now falling down her face. 'She never lost patience with me, and I want to help her. She has been through so much...'

'Rose, its ok. You have every right to want to protect your friend,' he reassured her.

'Thank you for your understanding,' she said, swallowing back the tears and nodding her head.

'That's alright, Rose. And as to what happened, nothing happened. That's what she wouldn't allow me to explain,' he said, releasing her hand and running a hand down his face in anguish.

'Christ! If only she had given me the chance to explain instead of just running.'

Looking down at her, 'Why did you run?' he asked in a whisper, while knowing she couldn't hear him. 'Why didn't you trust me? Why?'

'I don't understand.' Rose said, watching him.

'You must have heard the talk about the new Lady of the house...'

'Your house?' she asked.

'Yes.'

'Yes, I heard one of the kitchen staff in the market saying she must be the child of the devil. Everyone talks about her.'

Of course they did, he thought to himself. Nobody liked her and she was the talk of the town, how her husband put up with her he would never know. Maybe that's why he spent so much time away from home, he was staying out of her way.

'And trust me, Rose, that's not an exaggeration. I wouldn't be surprised if she was the devil himself,' he said.

'So, what of her?' Rose prompted, seeing him blow out a deep breath.

'The past few months she has set her eyes on me,' he said, looking straight into her eyes, hoping she would understand what he was trying to say. It was hard enough telling Emily, but she was more wise to the world, considering she came from the future, so therefore it didn't come as such a shock, but Rose on the other hand was still so innocent.

His hopes however were instantly dashed the moment she said, 'I don't understand.'

Taking a deep breath, he leaned forward with his elbows on his knees.

'She has been coming into my room, when knowing I would be there...'

Rose still looked blank, so he continued.

'At a time when she knew I would probably be getting changed,' he said, raising his eyebrows silently begging her to understand. He was greatly relieved to see that understanding finally dawned on her, and he saw her eyes grow wide and her bottom lip drop.

'But why? She's a married woman.'

'Why do you think, Rose?' he said, raising his eyebrows. She did ask some silly questions sometimes, he thought to himself and instantly felt guilty for thinking it.

'She came to my room again when she found out I was leaving, she must have been listening in when I was telling the lord I was leaving. Anyway, we were arguing when we heard a crash outside my room, and the instant she saw the door handle turning she grabbed me by my shirt, pulling me down with her on to the bed.'

Rose gasped, she was obviously shocked at what she was hearing.

'That crash outside, do you think it was Emily?' she asked, looking back down at her friend's bruised face.

'Yes, I think it was. I put my suitcase with our stuff outside the room, all ready for us to go. She must have not seen it and tripped, breaking her nose. There was blood on the floor outside the room and a lot of it. Plus, the suitcase wasn't where I put it,' he said, staring into space and seeing it all again. The blood, her face, her eyes, that look in her eyes when she walked into the room would forever haunt him until the day he died.

'Then she walked in seeing the two of you on the bed together,' she said.

Nodding his head because words weren't needed.

'Oh Emily,' she sighed, looking down at her friend.

'You must have thought history was repeating itself,' she said, with fresh tears in her eyes.

This drew his attention. Did she know something he didn't? Because it was a rather strange thing to say.

'What do you mean by that?' he asked.

'I guess she never told you,' she said, looking up at him.

'Tell me what?' he asked, frowning now.

'Before she came here, in her time, it was how she found out the man she was with was unfaithful. She walked into their home to find him in bed with another woman,' she said, going slightly red in the face and unable to look Henry in the eyes.

'Oh God!' he said, putting a hand to his mouth.

It all made sense now, why she reacted the way that she did, despite him telling her everything the night before. It was what Rose had said, she must have thought that history was repeating itself.

Well, history wasn't repeating itself and it never would.

He would find a way to convince her of that when she woke up, everything would work out, it would all be ok, it had to be, he told himself.

Chapter 12

Waking up and opening her eyes, she instantly felt like the ceiling was swirling round and round and with that feeling came another, just as equally unpleasant, nausea.

But it wasn't just the nausea, oh no, if it was just that she could have handled it, but her stomach felt like it was literally on fire!

Squeezing her eyes shut she became aware of another pain, putting a hand to her face she realised her nose was almost tripled in size, it was that swollen. If it was red as well, then she could definitely get a job as a clown, she thought.

And with that thought came the memory of how she got that big fat nose, her tripping up over that damn case and landing flat on her face, that's probably what gave her the giant nose.

Unfortunately, memories were like dominos, once one came down, they all came down, and in this case, it was the memory of seeing Henry on top of that woman.

It felt so strange though, as she felt like she couldn't quite remember everything so clearly, like watching a movie where it keeps clinching and moving to the next scene without playing out the previous scene.

And it was a feeling she wasn't used to.

It was her curse to remember everything, the amount of times when she was younger and she would get drunk and say or do something really stupid, like kissing someone in the toilets or trying to recreate the lift from dirty dancing, and that's just to name a few.

Thinking back, she could remember shouting and running, she grabbed a bottle of something, but in all honesty the second her lips had touched that bottle that's where the memory ended, it was a complete blank.

Putting her arms around her stomach, she groaned and that was when she felt a tender touch on her shoulder.

Opening her eyes, she instantly smiled at seeing Rose by her side.

'Hey,' she said, with a faint smile and realising it wasn't only her stomach which felt like it was on fire, but her throat too.

'Hi, how are you feeling?' Rose asked, looking worried.

She would have been concerned if Rose wasn't always worried.

'I feel awful,' she admitted, with a croaky voice. 'Can I have some water please? I sound like a frog.'

'Sure, here.'

Helping her sit up, she held a glass to her lips.

'Only take small sips for now, in case you're sick,' Rose warned.

The instant the cool water went past her lips and down her throat to her stomach, it felt like she had just drunk acid, and it was now burning her insides, and not to mention her stomach was now making some really unearthly sounds as if in protest.

'What the fuck!' she said, almost doubling over.

'I'll call the doctor, he's just in the other room,' Rose said.

Before she was able to take a step, Emily reached out in panic and grabbed her by the hand.

'Wait... Please don't leave me,' she said, with tears building up.

'Shhh... I am only going to the door to call him, he will hear me. I'm not going anywhere.' she said gently, putting a hand to Emily's cheek. 'Ok?'

Swallowing down a lump that quickly formed in her throat at the thought of being left alone, she nodded her head, afraid to speak in case she started to cry.

Sitting further up the bed and pulling her knees up to her chest so she could wrap her arms around them, she watched Rose open the door and call the doctor, informing him that she was now awake.

Looking around the room now, she realised she was in the doctor's office and was currently in the bed he used to examine some of his patients.

Rose then hurried over to her side and sat down in a chair beside her, taking hold of her hand and Emily held on back, not wanting to let go.

Rose must have seen the emotion on her face because she instantly stood up and pulled her against her where Emily quickly began to cry, not able to hold in.

She was hit with so many different emotions, she was scared, hurt, both physically and mentally and she was angry, angry at herself, at Henry, that woman and at the whole god damn world.

Why did fate bring her here just to make her suffer all over again? It wasn't fair.

When her tears had finally subsided, she heard a cough and realised the doctor was in the room and by her bed.

How long he had been standing there for, she had no idea.

Pulling back and looking up at her friend, she saw that she too had tears running down her face, which she wiped away and gave her a smile and a kiss on the top of her head.

Taking a step back with Emily still trying to hold on to her hand, the doctor said,

'It's ok, Rose, you can stay,' gesturing to the chair beside the bed.

Sitting back down, she held on to her hand which made Emily want to cry all over again. Christ, but she was so emotional, she had never cried so much in her life.

Taking a seat in the other chair, the doctor took her hand.

Looking down, she realised he was checking her pulse.

'How are you feeling, my dear?' he asked.

'Ok,' she replied, with a timid smile and a tremor in her voice because she was trying to hold it together and not cry again.

The doctor just smiled at her, obviously not believing her.

If she was truly ok, then she wouldn't be here now, would she?

'Ok,' he replied.

It was just something which was ingrained in her and probably the majority of people out there too, especially in her time.

When asked if ok, you just smile and say yes, no matter how you really felt inside, because nobody really wants to know your despair, they just pretend, in order to be polite.

That's just what the world had done to people, everybody just walked around holding on to their own fears and pain.

A perfect example of that was social media. You could put two different pictures up, one where you're looking sad and crying, and another of you opening a bottle of champagne. And guess what, the picture with the champagne would get the most likes and people asking what you're celebrating, but no one would ask why you are crying.

It was a sad world, and in more ways than one.

Standing up and putting the stethoscope to his ears, he then proceeded to listen to her heart.

Once he finished there, he then placed it over her stomach to have a listen, although he didn't really need the stethoscope for that as her stomach was being very loud and clear.

And that was when she realised, she was no longer wearing the dress she had on yesterday, but instead it was a very baggy shirt.

Looking over at Rose with panic clear on her face.

'This shirt, Hen…'

'Shhh, its ok. It was me, only me,' she said, giving her hand a squeeze.

Taking a deep shuddering breath, she nodded her thanks to her friend.

'You were quite soaked my dear,' the doctor said, putting the stethoscope away and proceeding to check the whites of her eyes, her nose and asking how much pain she was in.

Once he finished examining her, he took his seat beside her and in a gentle voice, 'My dear, would you like to talk about what happened?' he asked.

All she could do was shake her head and in all honesty, despite being afraid to speak because she was still so close to tears, she really didn't know what to say to this man.

It was like getting caught drinking in the local park when you should have been in school, and you have to explain your actions to your dad. That's exactly how she felt even though she was a grown-up woman, and he wasn't her father!

This man had been so kind to her the past few months, she had come to think of him as a friend and didn't want to disappoint him.

'My dear, I'm only concerned because what you did was almost suicidal. What you drank and the amount you drank…' he said, shaking his head, unable to finish what he was saying.

'I know, I know, I'm so sorry,' she said, with tears flowing down her face after seeing the pained look in his eyes.

Taking her hand gently. '...it could have killed you. You're going to feel quite sick over the next few days, but luckily you will be ok. Thank God, young Henry found you in time and you vomited most of it,' he said.

'I'm sorry. I wasn't trying to kill myself,' she whispered.

She didn't want the doctor thinking that she tried to end her life.

Yes, she was stupid, but suicidal she was not!

Patting her hand and getting up, she saw his eyes were glazed with unshed tears.

'I will leave you be and come back later to check on you, but Emily...' standing by the door now, he turned to look at her, 'you should speak with him, because it really isn't what you think it was.' And with that he turned and left the room, closing the door behind him.

Lying back down, she looked up at Rose.

'What did he mean by that? That it's not what I think it is? Was he talking about Henry?' she asked.

Chapter 13

Waking up, she realised it must be night as the room was now in darkness apart from two small lanterns, one on the doctor's desk which was opposite the bed she was currently lying in, and another on the little table beside her bed, in which they both gave the room a warm and cosy glow.

She tried to move and noticed that her right hand felt heavy and after lifting her head slightly from her pillow, she saw Henry sitting in a chair by her side, holding on to her hand and fast asleep with his head resting right on top.

Well, that explained the heaviness then, at least she knew she wasn't having a stoke, she thought, remembering something she saw on the telly once about the signs of a stroke.

Although her face did feel weird though, but that was due to her falling flat on her face and breaking her nose. Putting a hand to her face, she felt the swelling around the bridge of her nose, but thank God it wasn't too painful anymore and the swelling seemed to have gone down a bit too.

Resting her head back down on the pillow, she decided not to move so as not to wake him. She still had some thinking to do.

She had been so convinced that Henry had cheated on her that she reacted in the only way she knew how, she ran off, got piss drunk on some weird shit and nearly killed herself in the process.

Which, by the way, that shit she drank should be illegal, which it probably was in her time, she thought to herself, remembering that first taste and gagging. That stuff was enough to put off any alcoholic from drinking, for life! she thought, shuddering.

But after hearing a few things from Rose, she came to realise that she had in fact put two and two together and came up with bloody one hundred and five, way off the mark.

Remembering the conversation they had, after the doctor had left the room earlier, or was it yesterday? Honestly, she had lost track of time. It just felt like she was sleeping all the time and it still didn't feel like it was enough.

Rose had explained that Henry had informed her and the doctor of the harassment he had been enduring and explained what had happened that day, which admittedly he could have lied to them about, but she also informed her that Henry had been to see the doctor a few days ago, and she had overheard them speaking about a new job for him.

And so, the reason why that god damn case was outside his room that day was because he had packed their belongings and they were leaving, to start a new life together.

She knew what Rose had said made sense, about the reason the case was outside the door, unless it was actually her things, and she was being kicked out. But no, that didn't make sense and besides, Rose would never lie to her.

And why would he even be here now if it was all a lie, if he didn't care? He wouldn't be here holding her hand the way he was and sleeping by her side.

She needed to speak to him, find out from his own lips what had happened.

Shifting in the bed slightly as the back of her head was now beginning to feel a bit sore, no doubt probably due to the many hours lying on her back sleeping.

Pulling her hand back slowly, he lifted his head sleepily and the instant he saw that she was awake he became fully alert, sitting up in the chair.

Pulling herself up into a sitting position, he looked as if he wanted to help but had thought against it.

'Would you like some water?' he asked instead.

'Yes, please.'

She felt so thirsty, all she wanted to do was stick her mouth under a tap and drink until she felt like a balloon.

Getting up and pouring her a glass from a pitcher on the little table beside the bed, he handed it to her.

'Thanks,' she whispered, taking it with a slightly shaky hand.

She remembered Rose telling her to only take small sips in case she was sick, but she didn't feel sick anymore, just bloody thirsty!

So, she very quickly downed the glass of water and almost instantly regretted it, as she had to pull her knees up against the sudden and very painful cramp in her stomach.

Seeing her discomfort, he quickly took the glass from her hand and placed it back on the table.

'Are you ok? Should I call the doctor?' he asked, with concern clear on his face.

'No, it's just a cramp. It will pass,' she said, now wrapping her arms round her stomach and gently pressing against the pain as if it would help.

'It feels like my stomach literally decided to pull a fist,' she said, with a shaky voice and a slight smile on her face.

She wanted to downplay it a bit but at the same time she was scared shitless.

She had always been the type that scared easily, if there was a virus going around, she was always scared of catching it and would even somehow convince herself that she was actually sick.

Like this one time when her big toe suddenly went numb and after mentioning it to Craig, the fucker told her it was probably something serious, and she might need her toe to get chopped off if it wasn't treated quickly. And what did she do? She fucking fell for it, and booked herself an appointment to see the GP, about her bloody toe!

Now what she was afraid of, was spontaneous human combustion!

She watched a programme on the telly once about it and it always started in the abdomen, something about fat burning like a candle and whoosh, you were up in flames, burning from the inside out.

At that point her stomach decided to start making those groaning sounds again and for some reason that didn't make sense, she felt embarrassed by it and ended up tensing her muscles to try and get it to stop, which only made the cramp worse.

'The doctor said you would be in some discomfort for a few days,' he said, trying to reassure her.

'Discomfort! It feels like my insides are bloody burning!' she said, while thinking "typical men" while the images from that programme were flashing before her eyes. There was always a leg, usually from the knee down left behind, the rest of them was ashes.

'Why did you do it?' he suddenly asked, sitting back down.

'Do what?' she asked, confused what he was talking about.

'Why did you drink that whole bottle?'

'I...'

'Why did you run?' he asked, not taking his eyes from hers.

Did he seriously just ask her that? she thought, staring back at him in disbelief.

'Why do you think?' she asked, shaking her head.

'Because I saw you kissing her, that why,' she added.

'That's not what happened...'

'Oh, really? Then what did happen? Because where I was standing that's exactly what it looked like,' she said, staring daggers at him and feeling slightly guilty at the same time, but just the image of them both like that on the bed, just made her so damn angry.

'Emily...'

'What? Did you trip and fall on top of her?' she said, sarcastically.

Putting a hand to the back of his neck and looking up at the ceiling, he blew out a long breath.

He wasn't stupid, he could clearly see she had some major trust issues and after learning why from Rose, he couldn't exactly blame her. Anybody would have trouble trusting again after being treated that way.

But she could trust him, damn it!

'Do not judge me on the behaviour of others,' he said quietly, looking back at her.

'What's that supposed to mean?' she asked, frowning.

'I'm talking about the man you used to be with.'

'Craig?'

He nodded his head.

'How do you...'

'Rose told me,' he said, before she even finished the question.

Why she even bothered to ask was just plain stupid because she already knew the answer, it wasn't like she had many friends in whom to confide, now, was it? Just the one, Rose.

Although the whole of London probably already knew by now, back in her time that is. Things like that never stayed secret, not for long anyway, especially when the other woman was like the village bicycle, everybody got a ride.

'Great,' she muttered under her breath.

'Please don't be angry with her. She was defending you,' he said, suddenly looking worried.

'I'm not angry with her, I could never be angry with Rose.'

And that was the truth, Rose was the most innocent, sweetest, kindest person she had ever met, the girl didn't have a bad bone in her body. How could anyone ever be angry with someone so pure? 'I'm not even angry with you, not anymore anyway,' she said quietly, looking down at the bed.

'Emily...' He reached for her hand, where she was tracing a pattern on the bedsheet with her finger, but she pulled it back, resting it on her lap instead.

'Please, let me explain. It really isn't what you think. I promise. And deep down, I think you know that too,' he said, almost pleading with her to listen.

Rose had already explained to her what had happened, or more to the point what he said had happened and she trusted her friend, she didn't think for one second that she might have lied to her. But Henry certainly could have lied to Rose, knowing how sweet and innocent she was but he wouldn't be able to lie to her. She could smell a rat a mile away and she had Craig to thank for that, for giving her the experience.

Henry had been right though, when he said she knew the truth deep down, because somewhere deep down inside, she knew he was innocent.

But she had to be sure.

Because the heart and mind didn't always agree with one another, where one was all about the feelings and the gut instinct, the other wanted to be all logical and that was the one that wanted Henry to explain, so it could play spot the difference with the story she had already heard from Rose.

She didn't need to say anything, just her silence was enough for him to know that she was ready to listen.

'Thank you,' he said, and she could see the relief on his face.

'You remember the day I told you everything that had been happening with the mistress?'

How could she forget? she thought, while nodding her head, letting him know she still remembered.

'Well, that day, in the morning, in fact, before I even mentioned anything to you, I came here to ask the doctor if he knew of any jobs going. Then yesterday morning he informed me that a friend of his wanted a handyman and the job came with a little cottage on the grounds. There was even a job for you too, of course, if you wanted it that is, his wife just had her first baby and wanted some help. It was perfect for us...'

Hearing this, she had to fight to keep the tears down, because it did sound so perfect, but the question she was asking herself was, was it all gone now, or could they still have that perfect life Henry wanted for them, that she wanted for them.

'After going there with the doctor and meeting them and seeing the cottage that was to be ours, I went back to the house and packed a bag which I left outside the room all ready to go...'

'The bag I fell over smashing my face,' she said, putting a hand to her nose and wincing slightly at the pain while thinking so far so good, the story matched with what Rose had told her.

'Yes, I do apologise for that, but in my defence, I did not think that you would not see it.'

'Are you calling me blind?' she asked.

'No, of course not,' he said quickly with panic quickly settling in. 'I just meant that it's a big bag.'

At this point she just sat up straighter, crossed her legs and raised her eyebrows at him.

'Anyway...' he said continuing quickly, 'the mistress came into my room and asked what my bag was doing outside, she assumed that you alone were leaving.'

'Yeah, 'course she did. Bet the bitch was the moon.'

'That she was, for a short while that is. When I informed her that we were leaving together, she had tried to blackmail me...'

'Blackmail you, how?'

'She said she knew you weren't my sister, said she saw the way we look at each other and that she would tell the whole town, ruining your reputation. When I told her that wouldn't matter because we were soon to be wed, she said she would inform the police that you stole from her...'

'What?' She couldn't believe the lengths that woman would go to for a man who didn't even want her. What a bitch!

'Yeah, I told her if she did that then I would tell her husband what she had been up to...'

'Go on, Henry,' she said, impressed with how he stood up to her. It was about time too.

'Then she asked me why I would even want someone like you when I could have a real woman like her.'

'What? The bloody cheek. What did you say when she said that?' she asked.

She was beginning to feel the anger building up, if she ever saw that woman again, she didn't think she would be able to control herself. Women like her needed to be taught a lesson, a fist to nose lesson.

'Nothing. I didn't get the chance. That was when we heard you outside,' he said, blowing out a breath and shrugging his shoulders.

'And the rest is what you already know. Or saw should I say? We both knew it was you because we heard you swearing and when she saw the door opening, she grabbed me and fell back pulling me with her. I wouldn't have fallen so easily but she caught me off guard, I wasn't expecting her to do something like that,' he said, shaking his head and taking her hand in his, he kissed the back of her hand.

'I'm sorry for what she did, I'm sorry for what it looked like, I'm sorry for what it did to you and most of all I'm sorry from the deepest part of my heart that I allowed that to happen.'

And there it was, honesty. She could see it in his eyes, hear it in his voice, feel it in her gut. Plus, the story matched, something her mother had taught her when she was a kid, the way to catch someone out with a lie is to get them to retell the story. Because a liar could never remember the original lie as they first told it, kind of like the game Chinese whispers you played as a kid, what ends up coming back round to you isn't what you originally sent out.

This man before her now was the true victim in this sorry story, he had endured months of harassment from that woman, too afraid to say anything in case he lost his job, his home and just when he found happiness it was nearly taken away. Because let's be honest, if it wasn't for Rose, she probably wouldn't have given him the chance to explain.

She looked down at his hand holding on to hers and gave it a little squeeze back.

'I'm sorry,' she said, in barely a whisper.

'For what?' he asked, and when she didn't answer he gave her hand a little shake. 'Hey, talk to me, please.'

'For acting like a crazy woman and yelling at you. For running away, for not trusting you,' she said, now looking at him.

And she meant every word, she was sorry, she should have trusted him. After all, not all men were the same, she learnt that the day she met this man, he was a good, honest, hardworking man and she didn't want to lose him.

Cupping her cheek with his free hand, 'No, my sweetheart, you have nothing to be sorry for. I understand,' he said, tenderly.

Getting up, he came to sit on the edge of the bed beside her and leaning in, gave her the most beautiful tender kiss she had ever experienced. It was so light it felt like a feather just glided across her lips.

Resting his forehead against hers, he breathed in deep, as if he needed her scent as much as he needed oxygen.

If anything had happened to her, he didn't know what he would have done with himself. This woman was the other half of his soul.

'So, are we ok, then?' she asked slowly.

Hoping that, yes, they were going to be ok, and nothing would change or come between them ever again.

Pulling back just enough to look at her, 'I should be asking you that,' he said with a smile.

'But yes, for me nothing has changed, you have done nothing wrong. And nothing would ever change the way I feel about you, nothing. I love you, you are my heart and soul,' he said, looking into her tear-filled eyes and kissing her.

It was a slow, deep kiss she had always read about in books and longed to experience but never did, until now that was, because she was finally experiencing that perfect, soul consuming kiss.

'I love you too,' she whispered back.

❖

Chapter 14

Waking up the next morning, she found Henry was still by her side and in the very same position she had found him in the night before, head on her hand and fast asleep.

It gave her a warm tingle inside knowing that he cared enough to have put his own comfort to the side and spent the whole night by her side, sleeping in a chair. With the memory of him saying he loved her plastering a huge grin on her face.

Just then the door opened, and in walked the doctor who was closely followed by Rose, who quickly ran around him and to her side, the instant she saw she was awake.

'You're up! Oh, you look so much better. Doesn't she look better?' she said, looking back at the doctor excitedly.

'She does indeed, my dear,' he said, with a smile and coming over to her side. Giving Henry a pat on the back, who had just woken up, no doubt due to Rose's very loud and excited screeching.

'I do feel so much better,' she said.

'And how does stomach feel today?' the doctor asked.

'She was in a lot of pain last night, sir,' Henry said quickly, sounding worried.

Rose took hold of her hand and smiled while raising her eyebrows and nodding her head in Henry's direction, no doubt thinking the same as her, "Oh, bless".

'That's nothing to be concerned about Henry, it's to be expected considering everything,' giving him a smile and another pat on the back.

Turning his attention back to Emily, 'You will be in some discomfort for a few days and maybe some nausea, but it will soon settle. I'm happy to say that you're ready to go home. Do you have any questions, my dear?' he asked.

'Erm… No, I don't think so.'

'Thank you, sir,' she added, feeling the need to show this man the proper respect he was used to and deserved.

'Call me Edward, my dear,' he said, smiling down at her and patting the hand that Henry had finally let go off.

'Thank you, Edward,' she said with a smile.

'It's always a pleasure to look after a beautiful lady… Henry…'

'Yes sir?' instantly sitting up to attention.

'You can take Emily to her new home when you're ready, and I will be round in a couple of days to check up on you,' he said, directing this last part towards Emily. 'And in the meantime, if you need anything, you know where I am.'

And with a nod, he left the room.

'I'm so happy you two are still together,' Rose said, almost bouncing up and down with happiness while holding Emily's hand to her own chest.

How did she know they were still together?

'Were you eavesdropping again?' she asked, with a smirk.

To which they all heard the doctor from the other room call out, 'It's Rose's favourite pastime, didn't you know?'

She looked at Rose who just shrugged her shoulders. 'Sorry, I can't seem to help myself,' she said, not looking sorry at all.

Making Emily laugh and pulling her friend down for a big, long hug, this girl was an angel, and she didn't know what she'd do without her. She hoped her new home wasn't too far away, and she could still see her friend often.

Reluctantly breaking off the hug, 'I have something for you,' she said and left the room.

Shortly coming back with a fresh change of clothes for Emily, before leaving the room again and taking a very reluctant Henry with her, to allow Emily to get dressed in peace.

Poor Henry, he really didn't look happy leaving her side, she thought, shaking her head and laughing to herself at the image of Henry muttering, 'But we are to be wed soon.' And Rose pushing him out the room saying, 'Well, you're not married yet.'

Once dressed, she looked down at herself and for the first time since coming here she didn't miss her jeans and trainer, she actually felt like a lady.

Of course, it did help that they were brand new and the dress was a lovely pale blue colour, with a white frilly collar and white buttons on the front, leading down to where her belly button was. Even the boots were new. Pointing her foot out and looking down at them, she saw they were white with silk laces on the front and a little heel.

She absolutely loved the whole outfit.

Hearing a knock on the door, 'Come in.'

Upon seeing Rose entering the room she did a little curtsy and smiled.

'Thank you,' she said, knowing that this outfit came from Rose.

'Oh, I'm so glad you like it,' she said, clapping her hands together towards her chest and looking her up and down.

'Like it? Are you kidding me, I love it!' she said, doing a little twirl and looking down at herself and the way her skirt flowed around her.

'I'm so glad it fits, I was a little worried about you know...here,' she said, indicating to the boob area.

'Yeah, I know, they're like water melons, aren't they?' she said, laughing and looking down at her own boobs. Thinking how she had always struggled to find tops that fit perfectly, they were either too tight around the boobs or just perfect but too baggy around her tummy.

But this dress was perfect.

'It's perfect Rose, thank you. But this must have cost you a fortune, though, you must let me know how much it is, so I can repay you,' she said, making Rose draw in a sharp breath.

'You will do no such thing, Miss. This is a gift and one that suits you greatly, may I add?'

'Why, thank you,' Emily said again, adding in a curtsy just for fun.

'But hey, what's with the Miss, you'd stopped calling me that for a while.'

'Sorry... it's just that, dressed like that you kind of look like one of them,' she said, sheepishly.

And Emily knew exactly what she meant by "them".

'I'll let you in on a little secret,' she said, going closer to Rose.

'There's nothing ladylike about me,' she said behind her hand.

'For once I think I fully agree with you,' Rose replied, with a very serious expression and they both laughed.

'Come on, let's go show the others,' she said, linking her arm through Emily's.

✻✻✻

Several weeks had passed since they moved here to their new home, and exactly six weeks since they became husband and wife.

She would remember that day until the day she died, the day he proposed.

Walking into the kitchen at the doctor's house with Rose by her side, she didn't find Henry sitting at the table like she had expected. No, instead she found him down on one knee, holding out a ring.

Rose had unlinked her arm from hers and slowly nudged her forward with a smile on her face while stepping quietly back.

Looking down at that man, that amazing, wonderful man, she felt her heart begin to beat faster, her breathing coming quicker and a strange fluttering in her belly, the kind you got when you were going on a first date.

And if she had to guess, she would say that he felt the same way, as she could see that the hand holding out the ring wasn't exactly very steady.

And then he said it, the words she had always longed to hear,

'Emily, will you do me the honour of becoming my wife?'

And without hesitation and with a tremor in her voice, she said, 'Yes, yes,' while nodding her head and feeling the tears building up. Again.

And that was that, in a week they had been married in the local church with Edward and Rose as the witnesses.

It had been the most perfect day and everything she had wished it to be, she had never wanted a big fancy wedding with loads of people she didn't actually like, and they didn't like her; most of the time people only turned up at weddings for the free booze.

But this had been perfect, just her and the man she was to spend the rest of her life with, and their two friends.

Right after the ceremony they went back to the doctor's house where Rose had surprised them with a big feast she had prepared beforehand, where they ate and drank and even Rose got a little tipsy and had to be helped upstairs to her room.

Looking now at the wedding band on her finger and rolling the ring around with her thumb.

It was a little big and she was constantly worried about losing it, but Henry had assured her that they would get it re-sized, just as soon as they could afford it. She really hoped that would be soon.

Looking over at her friend who was happily tucking into the homemade scones and jam, she smiled when seeing the little blob of jam at the corner of her mouth.

It was a lovely sunny afternoon and Rose had come by like she always did on Sundays, with her famous homemade scones while Emily provided the jam. It was a little lumpy but tasty nonetheless, so not bad for her first attempt at jam making.

This is the life she thought, taking a deep breath and looking around her little garden while drinking her tea and watching Henry clipping away at some roses in the corner. They both had the day off as they usually did on Sundays, unless there was something urgent needed which couldn't wait until Monday.

This proved to be the best thing for Henry as their new employers turned out to be a really lovely couple with a new-born baby girl, not much older than herself and Henry, in fact.

And while Henry went about his various duties on the grounds, her job was to carry out some light cleaning, nothing major, just some dusting and sweeping but she quickly came to realise it was more for the mistress to have some company as she didn't go out much. Which was understandable, with a new-born baby and with her husband gone all day, she was home pretty much on her own all day.

Looking back at Rose now, 'Did you put anything in that locket yet?' she asked, pointing to the necklace around her friend's neck.

It was a beautiful gold-plated brass locket with a little black bird in mid-flight over a little red flower, which she had gifted to Rose the very next day after receiving her first wage.

Rose had done so much for her, and she knew that the beautiful dress she had got for her must have cost her entire savings.

She had the most purest, kindest soul and she deserved something in return.

'I don't have anything to put in it,' she admitted, finishing her scone and wiping her mouth.

She could imagine how hard that could be for Rose, because even in her time it was hard putting a photo inside a locket because they were usually so tiny, and photos didn't come in locket sizes.

Just as she was thinking this, a thought suddenly came to mind, and picking up one of the knives from the table, she cut a small lock of her hair.

Reaching out towards Rose, she opened the locket and put the lock of her hair inside before closing it back up again.

'There,' she said, with a smile, 'Now you can always have a piece of me with you.'

'By my heart,' Rose added, touching the locket.

***

After spending a lovely afternoon together, Henry suggested they take Rose home together and then take a little stroll together in the fields to check on their little willow tree.

She immediately jumped at the chance, and thought a little stroll to their favourite spot was the perfect opportunity to have a chat with him about something that had been on her mind for a couple of weeks now.

She realised about two weeks ago that she had missed her period, fair enough, she hadn't been keeping track of them like she used to, as she didn't have a working phone anymore where she could use the cycle app like she used to, and she hadn't been writing them down either.

But who could blame her with everything that had happened? She had literally been thrown into a new world.

But by some rough calculations in her head, she figured she should have had her period by now, it felt like quite a while since she last had one.

She wasn't exactly sure if indeed she was pregnant, it wasn't like she could pop to a pharmacy and get a pregnancy test now, was it? Because they didn't exist!

She decided to wait a little longer and if nothing happened, then she would go and see Edward. Rose however, suggested that she speak to Henry and assured her that he would be over the moon.

Dropping Rose off home and after having a little catch up with Edward, they walked hand in hand to the fields, where they found their little tree growing nicely, it even had a few little fresh leaves on it now.

Sitting down next to it in silence, they held hands.

She really enjoyed these moments with Henry. Silence with him was never awkward, it was comfortable, it was as if their souls spoke to each other without them needing to use words.

Watching him look out towards the crops, she asked, 'Do you miss it? Working here, I mean.'

'No. Why do you ask?' turning round to look at her.

'Oh, it's nothing. Just the way you were looking, that's all,' she said, rubbing little circles on her hand with his thumb.

'I was just thinking back to the day I met you, it was right there,' he said, pointing out just in front of them.

'You mean the day I fell from the sky and straight into your arms like an angel,' she said, with a cheeky grin and a wink.

'Well, I wouldn't put it like that exactly. You puked in my arms and sweetheart, there was nothing angel like about you,' he said. 'And did I mention that you also peed yourself?' he added.

'Heyyy,' she said, trying to pull her hand free from his grip which he only tightened in protest, pulling her closer and planting a hard kiss on her lips, before tucking her into his side and putting an arm around her.

'Ok, you're forgiven,' she said, making him laugh.

Putting an arm across his middle, she held on tight, taking a deep contented breath.

'I like it when you call me "sweetheart",' she admitted.

'Well, you are my sweetheart and always will be,' he said, kissing the top of her head.

After a few moments of silence between them, she said,

'Can I ask you something?'

'Anything my love.'

Smiling, 'I love it when you call me that too.'

'My sweetheart, my love, my sunshine…'

'Anything but an angel though,' she said, interrupting.

'Or a lady for that matter.'

'Yeah, I can't argue with that one,' she said, and they both laughed.

'What did you want to ask me?'

Ok, here goes she thought to herself.

'What do you think of children?' she asked, thinking it wasn't a bad idea to test the waters first.

'Oh, I love them. I want to have loads.'

'What is loads exactly?' she asked, while thinking she wasn't a rabbit who could produce five or six at once.

'I don't know, maybe twelve.'

'What! Why twelve?' she asked, pulling back and sitting up straight to have a better look at him.

'I don't know, I guess I just like the number.'

'Well, I like the number fifty, it doesn't mean I want fifty kids!'

To which he started to laugh, prompting her to narrow her eyes at him.

'You're winding me up, aren't you?' she said, seeing that cheeky glint in his eyes.

'Of course, I am,' he said, laughing and pulling her back to him.

'I'll settle for ten,' he said.

And he got a playful punch in the belly in response.

'How many do you want?' he asked.

'I've always wanted three. A boy and two girls, the boy being the eldest so he can protect his sisters,' she answered back.

'That sounds like the perfect number,' he said, resting his head on top of hers.

Well, so far so good, she thought, at least she was now sure he wanted kids.

But she still felt nervous, no doubt due to the psychological trauma carried over from her previous train wreck of a relationship.

Taking a deep breath, here goes she thought, 'I think I might be pregnant,' she said quietly and quickly, looking straight ahead, too afraid to look up at him in case she saw a reaction she didn't want to see.

Pulling himself back and turning to face her, 'You're pregnant? With a baby?' he asked with a tremor in his voice.

'Erm… yeah, a baby. What else?' she said.

Bless his little heart, she thought to herself.

'A baby,' he repeated to himself, staring out into the distance, while she watched his face with bated breath.

And just like that he reached out, pulling her towards him with the momentum taking them both down, ending with her landing on top of him with a squeal.

'We're pregnant!' he said, wrapping both arms around her.

And if his reaction was anything to go by, she could safely and happily say that he was happy with the news. Although happy seemed to be an understatement, the man was obviously overjoyed, and it made her heart sing.

'You do realise that I'm the one who's pregnant, right? That it's physically impossible for men to be pregnant,' she added, while he was nuzzling her neck, making her laugh.

She knew full well what he meant but it was still funny winding him up.

Grabbing her head in both his hands, 'We're pregnant!' he said again, out loud this time with obvious joy, making her laugh.

Apart from her wedding day, this was her second happiest moment in her life, and she already knew that the third would be the day she gave birth to Henry's child.

Placing her head down to his chest, she took a deep breath, wishing she could freeze this moment forever.

Then a thought entered her mind which was enough to dampen her mood, but not for long.

'I just wish you could stay with me, during the labour I mean. I know things are different here…'

'Sweetheart, nothing and I mean absolutely nothing will keep me away. I will be by your side every step of the way.'

'But what about…'

'Don't worry about anything my love. Besides I'm sure Edward would relax the rules for us,' he said, instantly making her relax.

Because he was right, Edward would relax the rules for them because he knew where she was from and besides if he didn't, she always had Rose. But it was enough to know that Henry wanted to be there.

'You have made me the happiest man alive,' he whispered into her hair with a shaky voice and in her current position of lying on top of him, she felt him take in a rather shaky deep breath.

'Are you crying?' she asked, secretly enjoying this side of him.

'No,' he said, quickly. Bringing a hand up to his face, no doubt to wipe away a stray tear before bringing it back down on to her back, where he was now running a hand up and down her back in a slow caressing motion, the sensation making her arch her back slightly, 'And you have made me the happiest woman alive.'

Opening her eyes, she realised they must have both dozed off, although not for long as it was still light.

Looking up she saw that there was obviously a storm brewing but what got her heart racing was the way the clouds were rolling in the sky. They moved exactly the same way they did the day she came here.

Sitting up and nudging Henry, 'Henry, wake up. We have to go, wake up.'

'Mmm, I'm up,' he said, opening his eyes. 'Did we fall asleep?' he asked groggily.

'Yeah,' she said, looking up at the sky and feeling a wave of panic building up.

'Henry, get up,' she said, when she saw him close his eyes again. 'Look at the sky.'

Opening his eyes, he now saw what she saw, and she could see the same panic mirrored in his eyes.

Getting up, he helped her to her feet.

'Don't worry, lightning doesn't strike twice in the same place, or so they say,' he said, shrugging his shoulders. But she could see the way he was eyeing those clouds now and she didn't like it.

'Let's go,' he said, taking her hand.

And with an iron grip on her hand, he began to walk quickly away, taking her with him.

They were halfway out of the fields when she realised her wedding band was no longer on her finger.

'Shit! My ring, it fell off.'

'Leave it, we'll get it later. Come on,' he said, pulling her behind him as she had slowed down.

She really didn't want to lose that ring, it was a symbol of their love, put on her finger in the house of God. What if they couldn't find it later, what if they couldn't come back later and someone finds it and takes it?

Like he said, lightning didn't strike twice in the same place, so really what were the chances?

Looking up at the sky, she felt the fear in the pit of her stomach. She would be quick she thought, it probably fell off at the willow tree.

Pulling her hand free from his grip, 'I'll be back in a second,' she said and started to run back before he could stop her.

'Emily...' he called after her.

'It's probably at the willow tree,' she called back over her shoulder while running.

'Leave it, come back,' he said and started running towards her.

'I have to find it...' she called out while looking frantically around her on the ground.

'EMILY...' he screamed.

The last thing she saw was Henry running towards her, eyes wide with panic. Screaming her name before she heard a loud crack, and everything went dark.

Chapter 15

Opening her eyes slowly, she felt that very familiar wave of nausea and spinning that she was strangely becoming accustomed to.

Feeling a touch on her hand, she smiled.

'Henry...' she said groggily, eyes half shut.

'No sweetie, it's Stace. Don't worry, I'm here, I'm not going anywhere, babe.'

Closing her eyes again, the last thought that went through her mind before going back to sleep was, shamefully, that it wasn't the voice she wanted to hear.

Waking up again, the first thing she noticed was that she was in a hospital, a very real and very modern hospital. Looking down at her left arm she saw she had a blood pressure cuff attached and a pulse reader on her finger, as well as a needle stuck in her arm which was attached to a bag of clear fluid.

Looking at all this she didn't need to be told what year it was.

Looking around the room she saw it was day, as light was streaming through the large windows that lined one side of the big room. And instantly the memory of Henry's old room, the light streaming through his little window that first day, flashed before her eyes.

Just then a nurse walked into the room making her jump.

'I see you're awake Miss Smith,' she said, glancing at something above her head.

Tilting her head up she saw a small white board above her bed with a name that no longer seemed familiar to her, "Emily Smith".

She was aware the nurse had said something and was obviously waiting for a reply, but she didn't quite catch what she said.

'Sorry?' she asked, looking back at her.

'Have you been awake long?' she repeated, watching her.

'Erm, I don't know. I don't think so, no,' she said, looking back up at the board.

'Ok, I will get the doctor once I'm done checking your vitals.'

Once she finished checking her blood pressure and temperature, she started to head towards the door.

'I will go get the doctor now, Miss Smith. Would you like me to also contact your next of kin, let them know you're awake?' she asked.

Miss Smith, that wasn't right. That wasn't her name, not anymore anyway, she thought to herself.

'Mrs Taylor,' she said quietly, almost to herself.

'Sorry? Is that who you want me to call?'

Looking up at her now, 'Mrs Taylor, that's my name.'

'Oh, I'm sorry. That's what we had on file and your next of kin...'

'I'm married,' she whispered.

'I'll go get the doctor,' she said with a kind smile, then left the room closing the door behind her.

She knew exactly what had happened, where she was or when she was to be more exact.

She also knew that she couldn't mention a word of it to anyone, especially the doctors as they would have her strapped up and put into a mental institution.

Looking down at her left hand she saw that there was no ring on her marriage finger, and that was because it fell off, and being the idiot that she is, she stupidly went back to get it despite Henry telling her not to.

Why? Why did she do that? Why did she run back? She should have stayed with Henry. If she had done what he said she wouldn't be here now, she would still be with the man she loves.

Why? Why? Why? She said out loud, angrily pulling at her finger where her ring should have been.

Feeling the tears begin to build and rise, she took a deep breath to calm herself, swallowing the tears back down while feeling the heaviness in her chest.

She didn't want to cry because she knew exactly what would happen if she did. If she allowed herself to start, she was afraid she would never stop and would indeed end up in a mental institution.

If she allowed herself to fall into a deep, dark pit of despair, she didn't think she had the strength to pull herself back up.

And the scary thing was, she knew she wouldn't even want to.

Henry was her love, her life, her everything. What did she have without him? Nothing.

How could she get back to him? And was it even possible again? Could he get to her?

All these questions started flowing through her mind when the door opened and in walked a man, followed by the nurse who was in earlier.

He was a tall, slim man with short blond hair, dressed in beige trousers and a Ralph Lauren pink shirt and everything about him including his face screamed that he couldn't be bothered, he was only in it for the money.

Unlike Edward. Who did what he did because he cared.

'I've just been informed we have the wrong name for you,' he said, coming to stand by the side of the bed and looking down at the clipboard in his hands.

'How are you feeling?' he asked, getting out a little slim torch and flashing it from one eye to the next, making her eyes water.

'Ok,' she replied, wiping her eyes.

What could she say? No, I'm not ok? My heart has been literally ripped out of my chest because I got struck by lightning and time travelled back here, leaving the man I love behind in a time I grew to love. And all I could think about is that one day I would die and hopefully there is an afterlife where his soul would be waiting for mine?

No, she didn't think so.

'Any headaches, double vision?'

'No.'

'Any palpitations?'

'No, nothing.'

'Good,' he said, while writing something on the clipboard he had.

'Well, I'm happy for you to go home. Now we've also taken some blood this morning but we're still waiting for the results, someone will give you a call once they come in if anything shows up, but I expect everything will be fine,' he said with a fake smile.

'Ok, thanks.'

Just as he reached the door to leave, she remembered that she didn't have a phone anymore.

'Sorry, excuse me. I don't have a phone anymore, it broke...'

'No problem, we'll give a call to your next of kin. Erm... Stacy, with your permission of course.'

'Yeah, that's fine.' And speaking of the devil, just like that Stacy came walking in.

'Omg, sweetie. I was worried sick,' she said, running over and pulling her into a big, long hug.

'Are you ok? You gave me such a fright,' she said, once she released her, holding her at arm's length in order to look her up and down.

'Do you have a fever? Because you look a little red,' she asked, putting a hand to her forehead.

And with that action she was instantly transported back to the day in the fields, when Rose had done the exact same thing when she had called herself a fool.

Again, she had to push down those damn tears that kept threatening to spill like lava out of a volcano, at least for now until she was alone.

'Did they say when you can go?'

'Yeah, he said I'm good to go.'

'That's brilliant! God, you had me so worried there for a minute. When that lightning hit you yesterday...'

'What?' What did she just say? She thought she heard her saying "yesterday" that wasn't right, she must have misheard.

'Say that again,' she said, when she realised Stacy was just staring at her.

'Erm... that you got struck by lightning,' she said slowly.

'No, I know that! When did it happen?' beginning to get impatient with her friend and annoyed at the nurse who had just pulled the needle out of her arm a little too roughly.

'Hey, watch it,' she said to the nurse. God, they treated people like animals in this place.

'Sweetie, calm...'

'Don't tell me to calm down. When did it happen? Tell me. Please,' she pleaded.

'It happened yesterday. Are you sure you're ok, sweetie? You've kind of gone white,' she said, but Emily was no longer listening. It just didn't make any sense, she was so confused. Was it possible it was all a dream? But no, it was real, she could feel it in her heart, in her soul.

'It can't be. It was real, I know it is,' she said in a whisper.

'What's real? Sweetie? Say something, you're scaring me now,' looking up at her friend and seeing the look of concern on her face, then at the nurse who was looking down at her over the rim of her glasses.

'It's nothing, let's get out of here,' she said.

***

Lying down on Stacy's sofa in a daze watching television, she couldn't believe the crap they put on in the daytime.

How did she ever watch this shit? she thought to herself, as she picked up the remote and turned it off.

Closing her eyes, she could see Henry's face as clear as day, as if he was right there in front of her.

She knew now that it wasn't all a dream, that it had been real, now how it had happened she had no clue, she would need a scientist to figure that one out.

But it had been real, and she had the evidence to prove it.

Sitting up, she put a hand to her belly remembering last night's conversation with the nurse who had called to discuss her results. And being told that her blood had detected HCG, which the nurse explained was a pregnancy hormone after she enquired what that was, thinking she had cancer or something just as bad.

So, she had been right when she told Henry and Rose that she thought she might be pregnant.

Putting her head in her hands and shaking it in disbelief.

And that dream, she thought, that dream she had of chasing a little boy around the willow tree, it suddenly made sense now. That willow tree or to be more exact that size of the willow tree only existed in this time, that dream hadn't just been a dream, it had been a premonition!

Getting up she walked over to Stacy's spare room and lay down on the bed, feeling both mentally and physically exhausted.

Suddenly something caught her eye on top of the chest of drawers, where Stacy kept a vanity mirror and some make-up.

But what got her heart jumping in her chest was a locket.

Getting up from the bed and walking over, she picked it off the mirror where it was dangling down, and her heart started to race like it was on a marathon. Because in her hand, she was holding the locket she had given to Rose!

Undoing the little clasp, she saw with a sinking heart that it was empty.

Later that night, curled up on the sofa with Stacy eating popcorn while watching a movie, curiosity had finally taken over and she asked.

'Where did you get that locket from?'

'What locket?' Stacy asked, with a mouthful of popcorn.

'The one in my room, it has a pretty little black bird on it.'

'Oh, that one. It's a family heirloom, it got passed down from a great great grandmother or something like that. Mum was gonna sell it at a car boot last year, when I saw it and saved it just in time. It's pretty, isn't it?' she said, adding. 'I remember mum saying my gran found a lock of hair in it when she was little,' she said, passing the popcorn towards Emily who declined, while looking at her friend.

That's it! She thought. That's why Rose had reminded her so much of Stacy and Stacy of Rose. They were related!

'I love you,' she found herself saying to her friend with tears in her eyes.

'Hey… I guess those pregnancy hormones are settling in already,' she said laughing and pulling her in to her side for a one-sided hug.

'I love you too, you, silly goose. Now have some popcorn coz I'm ruining my diet,' she added, kissing her on the side of her head.

Taking the popcorn, she put one in her mouth while smiling for the first time since she got back.

Epilogue

SEVEN MONTHS LATER

Heavily pregnant and about to pop, Stacy had managed to drag her out of the house and to a museum of all places.

At least it was nice and cool inside, she thought to herself, as she walked around, dreading going back outside in that god damn heatwave.

'I swear if one more person tells me the heat must be killing me, I'll punch them in the nose,' she muttered to herself, already on edge as Craig had pissed her off first thing in the morning.

He had the fucking cheek to come knocking on Stacy's door begging to be let in. He had heard about her being pregnant and came round to say that he would be there for her and the baby. She had to tell him he was a fucking moron as it couldn't possibly be his baby, because they didn't have sex in months!

It just went to show he didn't know who he was having sex with, he was always that high!

Stacy had made her laugh though as well as reminding her of Rose, because they said the exact same thing.

'You come here again, I swear I'll chop your fucking dick off,' she said, upon seeing him on her way back from buying croissants for their breakfast.

As she walked around looking at the ancient artefacts, one in particular had caught her eye, making her stop.

It was a phone, one of the first phones to be invented. But what had actually drawn her eye and almost caused her heart to stop beating, was the picture above the phone.

It was a picture of a man sitting in a chair and another man standing just beside him.

The man sitting was Edward and the man standing by his side was Henry himself!

Looking closer at the picture, at the face of the man she loved, she saw that he looked older and tired with slight wrinkles around his eyes where he didn't have before.

And around his neck was a chain, a chain with a single ring hanging from it. Her ring, her wedding band, the one she lost. He had found it, he kept it!

Looking at the date underneath the picture she saw it read 7 March 1876.

And with tears filling her eyes, she put a hand on her swollen belly and said with a catch in her voice,

'That's your father.'

THE END

www.ingramcontent.com/pod-product-compliance
Lightning Source LLC
Chambersburg PA
CBHW070948180726
48291CB00004B/1192